Renier-Fréduman Mundil

Roxanna

The Fatal Secret of the Murder Books

Crime Novel

AF209159

Renier-Fréduman Mundil

Roxanna

The Fatal Secret

of the Murder Books

Crime Novel

Translated from German

by Hilary Teske

FSC
www.fsc.org
MIX
Papier aus ver-
antwortungsvollen
Quellen
Paper from
responsible sources
FSC® C105338

Bibliographic information from the German National Library:
The German National Library lists this publication in the German National Bibliography; detailed bibliographic data is available online at http://dnb.dnb.de.

© 2025 Renier-Fréduman Mundil, Viola Hartmann
Cover design: Ilka Cierpka, CIERPKAGRAFIK
Editing: Malin Friese
Publisher: BoD · Books on Demand GmbH,
Überseering 33, 22297 Hamburg, bod@bod.de
Print: Libri Plureos GmbH,
Friedensallee 273, 22763 Hamburg

ISBN: 978-3-8192-8045-0

Content

It begins with a murder, as befits a detective story, a somewhat bizarre female detective, events that take place in Rome, England and France. A story that jumps back to the Middle Ages, runs on two tracks, two suspicious women and a dead man who suddenly appears one night to one of the two suspects. Alive, of course, at least for a short time. Murder motives that don't want to reveal their secret and the simultaneous death of both suspects who, to make matters worse, are absolutely the only ones who could be responsible for the crime(s). A tangled criminal string that seems to have been partially untangled by diligent endeavors – only to become even more tangled in the next moment and finally, seemingly lying in front of you untangled in a perfectly straight line.

At least seventy dead years lay before her. Death had eaten everything, skin and hair, not completely, what remained was an old grey shell.

The carefree years of a childhood with the privilege of growing up on the magnificent estate – gone, devoured by death. The exciting years at school and later at boarding school. The adventurous confusion of puberty – gone, swallowed up by death.

The meeting with her first boyfriend, the pompous wedding, the initially blissful first years of marriage – gone, swallowed up by death. The late years of widowhood after her husband's death – gone, swallowed up by death, including the dead woman's many memories of her husband and her daughter M.

The later flare-up of the flame of life through acquaintance with a messenger, the love literally carried into the house by a messenger, devoured by death. Everything has disappeared. Except for the grey shell. Everything grey, starting with her hair, once an ebony snow- white-like jet-black. Grey the wrinkled skin, the toenails, exposed by the light sandals, grey, striped dark grey.

Roxanna's life experiences were enough to easily imagine the grey dead shell as an elegant, almost tall, fine woman with slightly curly, jet-black hair, with an elegant gait and an upright head. The dead woman had once been all this. Now she lay on the floor in front of her as a grey-faced, frozen, cold shell.

A huge black shadow weighed on the southern side of the splendidly majestic building. Picturesque figures were enthroned on the marble plinths of the magnificent building, their faces bathed in the glistening sunlight disappearing on the precious earthen floor in the huge shadow of the dome, only in a few places on the black surface dot-shaped bulges were formed as an earthen expression of the figures hovering between earth and sky. Their protruding feet, barely concealed by their stone robes, were skillfully fixed to the bases of the towers, an invisible force chaining the statues to their stone foundations to prevent them from gliding away into the sky. Their significance was concealed in their outward appearance in a magnificent yet unobtrusive manner, reminding the miniaturized inhabitants of the city to think of visions of a heavenly realm every day of their existence.

The medieval dignitary sat on a lavishly decorated balcony, balustraded with naked female images, entwined with strange creatures.

The weight of his body flowed seamlessly into the looming grandeur of the building, from time to time the hectic pace of a rushing servant interrupted the tranquility of captive time.

The dignitary held a gold-tipped telescope in his bulging hands and had directed it towards the earth at the angle of the sun's rays.

In the prisms of the glass, the image of a naked woman split apart, whirred through the dark corridor of the telescope and disappeared into the dignitary's eye with streams of sweet fragrance.

Behind the naked woman, years ago, a poor hut had erupted from the barren ground, nothing had changed about it over the years except for the decomposing traces of time, which gnawed at the building like destructive bacteria, letting it slide back into the immeasurable womb of Mother Earth as putrid rubbish.

The dignitary's eye rested for a long time on the naked female body. The woman performed ordinary tasks, as everyday life demanded. While doing housework, her body took on ever-changing postures, constantly raising other naked parts of her body, again parallel to the sun's rays falling from the sky, only this time in different directions.

The ringing of the huge bell, inside which the miserable hut would have found ample room, made the dignitary put the telescope aside. Fine rivulets of sweat had formed in his palms, confusing the end of the telescope with a stinking drain and coating the artistically crafted glass with a thin, slimy film.

Prepare the bed, the dignitary ordered his servant on his left, and the meal, I will eat it in bed.

With an envious look on his face, the servant hurried away, slipped out of the sumptuously balustraded airy room and disappeared into the cool chambers. For a few unobserved moments, he himself had let his eye slide through the telescope, focused on the same point, the same event, because it had been re-peating itself from day to day for several weeks.

A grey cloak, the fullness of which extended the red speckled hair, slipped from the slender shoulders of the woman's body and covered the floor with its hem. Two sparkling eyes broke out of the thick fringe of hair into the sun-drenched daylight and leapt across the spacious hall. They stopped in front of the bed. The massive figure of the dignitary rested on silk-covered feathers, wrinkled skin labored to hold the fullness of his intestines together. Next to the bed, the meagre remains of the eaten meal exuded the last sweet smells, strangely combining the naked figure of the dignitary with the grey-clad slender female body.

At a signal from the dignitary, servants hurried into the hall and removed the remains of the grey covering from the woman's skin. Their glances betrayed an inability to grasp the situation with adequate understanding. The woman's mind was confused, its enormous bizarreness not in the least inferior to her overwhelming beauty.

The dignitary beckoned her closer in a friendly manner. The skill of his doctors, who had sealed the woman's fertile tube with a slightly corrosive liquid, flashed through his mind at that moment. The dignitary groaned indifferently. The meal lay heavy in his guts and, following the force of gravity, began to migrate downwards. It took twice the effort for his aged body, at the level of the navel the blood flow divided, an extensive half flowed into the bulging intestines, the other half of the red-soaked lifeblood flowed a little further downwards.

An hour later, two servants entered the room and carried the sleeping woman outside.

The dignitary was disgusted when the woman's gently wheezing body nestled against him in the unconsciousness of sleep.

The exhausted woman only woke up again in her hut, sometimes her sleep-induced return was via the servant's room, and he scanned the hut for the naked woman's body with his master's telescope when a favorable opportunity arose. When the woman awoke, she saw the sumptuously set table. Invisible hands, under the control of the dignitary like every moving hand in the city, had filled the table. After sleep had receded, the woman fell upon the colorful table and greedily devoured the delicacies spread out before her. At the same time, fifty meters higher, closer to the sky, the exhausted dignitary rested for the next day.

Let's assume that you are still alive. You're not lying on the ground, your eyes directed downwards, into the cold earth. Your gaze is straight ahead, something, let's say someone, you see, someone must have met your gaze. Let's assume this person was like you, I mean female basic structure. Let's talk about age. Not your age, I mean, let's say this person was younger than you. Not a bad idea. The question is, how much, how many years younger was this person? Let's summarize: a female person, younger than you, maybe five, let's say six, six years younger than you. You can disagree with me if it's not true.

Don't you feel well? The young policeman looked at the female inspector. Strange creature, talking to herself.

I've rarely felt better, Roxanna replied, and I've never had a single conversation with myself in my entire life. I wouldn't even know how to address myself.

But you were just talking, interrupted the young officer, and there's nobody here except the dead woman.

I always talk to the victim. Do you know a better witness? I certainly don't. Young kid from the police academy, Roxanna mumbled to herself. Cheating death with dead textbook knowledge.

Do me a favor, Roxanna said in a firm tone. I prefer to talk to others at eye level. Do you understand?
The young policeman didn't understand, of course. But before he could question her back, his colleague

had rushed forward, bent down, reached under the dead woman with both arms and dragged the slowly freezing body into an armchair, right opposite Roxanna.

You still have a lot to learn, young man! Roxanna snapped at the newcomer from the police academy. Your colleague, look what ten years of professional experience can do!

She turned back to the older of the two.

Be so kind as to put a glass in the dead woman's hand. Water will do. I don't think she realizes the difference between water and whisky anymore. It could be a long conversation. A glass of water is good for her dry tongue. Whisky, murmured Roxanna, only to become louder immediately afterwards, whisky, since we're talking about alcohol: Was the dead woman preserved at an early age?

You mean an alcoholic?

I mean preserved at an early age, just like I said.

The two policemen shook their heads. There was a bar in every other room. A minibar in the bedroom, like in a hotel. The bottles were barely opened.

No travelling companion!

The older policeman bit his lips at this word. Too late. It had slipped out by mistake, he could have sunk into the ground.

Roxanna glared at him. With lightning speed, she reached for a glass, and it shattered at his feet with the clear sound of a bell.

Get out of here, she hissed at the careless man. The next glass will land on your head. And you know, even I can't have a conversation with two dead people at once.

The two policemen hurried out of the living room, where death had spread itself out cozily. Nothing of what they had heard about the inspector had been confirmed. It was far worse than their most unflattering expectations.

As calmly as a lover's hand, the Seine floated through the city. Melancholy accordion sounds torn from the dream dripped from the riverbank into the lazy water. Individual barges, wrapped in garlands, were carried away by the weak current. Laughing conversations ploughed through the air, bouncing against the people strolling along the banks and disappearing into people's heads through their open ears.

Behind the next bend in the river, the Seine squeezed through white sandy beaches. Beach chairs filled with kilos of stripped flesh dotted the beach. After sunbathing, reddened or even tanned bodies lay in the light-colored sand coating, wrapped provisionally in a few places with strips of cloth, as if to prevent them from falling apart.

Michelle's black hair was at least a meter long. She had skillfully decorated her head with it. Oversized sunglasses were perched on her long but delicate nose. Behind them were two blue Mauritius, the most precious eyes in the city. The rest of her body was covered by a wide sundress, and in a few places a velvety, even tan emerged. Delicate feet stuck halfway into the sand, where they absorbed the cold of the ground and transferred it to the overheated body.

Michelle Denatielle, if I'm not mistaken.

Just say Michelle. Denatielle, who likes to hear Denatielle.

Oui, oui, Michelle. May I sit with you?

I can't refuse you. I can't dispose of more than the square meter of floor I'm lying on.

It doesn't matter, said the visitor, at least that it's only one square meter here. In the city, the land should belong to you in hectares.

I didn't bother with it. But if nobody wants it. You see, land wants to be owned. All this talk of free land. Show me a handful of soil on this desolate globe that isn't crying out to be owned. Because eventually the next one will come. The quarrel is already there and the blood is flowing. You see, this lump of earth is devious. Promises itself to several people, only to suck up their blood at some point.

Philosophy at the Sorbonne, I presume. How long did you study there?

500 years of the Middle Ages. Interesting. The best period of a person's life. So also of history. Study the Middle Ages if you want to know something about yourself and the other eight billion bipeds.

The stranger looked down at the woman. She corresponded one hundred per cent to the image of a wealthy young woman who had no need to work, excluded from the sphere of protesting students by a well-meaning upbringing, occasionally attending meaningless parties in search of the best way to get a day over with as quickly as possible.

Romana Vaticana, said the stranger abruptly, as if taken out of context.

The young woman started. Her eyes glazed over as she stared into the stranger's face.

I imagined you differently, she babbled with a dry mouth. More southern, Italian, completely different.

But you completely fulfil my expectations. You see, it all evens out. You zero percents, me one hundred percents fulfilled expectations. That's fifty per cent each. Not a bad ratio.

Maybe, Michelle stammered. Let's go. My flat is less than two hundred meters from here. I have a lot of questions for you.

The stranger nodded. Answering questions was his job. It was a good living. Not enough to own a flat two hundred meters from the banks of the Seine. But still enough, instead of disappearing behind a grey factory gate day in, day out for forty years.

The two of them slipped away from the white beach, leaving the sluggishly murmuring Seine behind them, the conversations on the boats slowly died away and the two points merged with a flat on the fifth floor of the quiet street, including a view of the Seine.

After the third whisky, Roxanna broke off the one-sided conversation with the dead Madame Richaud. She had learnt enough, not enough to solve the case, but more than she could normally extract from the victims in such conversations. The dead woman looked at her with a frozen gaze, fueled by a shot of melancholy sadness. Roxanna stood on her slender feet and smoothed out her skirt, which had slipped a double hand's breadth – a man's hand, what else – over her knees due to the folds that had appeared. Now it ended an inch above the slightly protruding kneecap. Roxanna took a last sip of whisky, damn good stuff, her great-grandfather couldn't have distilled it better. Then she took the glass of water from the dead woman's hand. Not a trace of it had emptied.

When she turned round, a young man was standing behind her. She had no idea how long he had been in the room. A well-groomed three-day beard covered the man's face, his delicate hands ran nervously over his face.

Excuse me, the door was open.

What door? Roxanna asked.

The entrance. I mean at the front. The main entrance. Well, the front door.

Roxanna sensed the young man's nervousness. Only now did she notice the flat box in his hand, the sweet smell of onions emanating from the box.

I've brought the pizza for Madame.

You're too late, Roxanna replied curtly.

Too late? Has Madame already left?

Gone away? Where was she going?

I don't know. She always wanted to go away. Just not to stay at home. Sometimes she ordered a pizza just for the journey to the airport. To catch the next best plane.

The man seemed more familiar with the deceased than was usual for a pizza delivery man. Perhaps he also offered other services. Roxanna scrutinized him. The deceased had taste, she had to give her that.

What have you brought? the inspector asked unexpectedly.

Pizza with salami and peperoni. Without onions. They're in a separate box. She always ordered the same thing.

Pizza with salami, Roxanna repeated.

She hadn't had anything in her stomach since the morning. And the pizza wasn't evidence anyway.

Unpack it, she said dryly, I'll get us something to drink. I have a few questions for you. Besides, you're hungry. I can see it in your face.

The young man silently followed her instructions while Roxanna disappeared into the dining room. She opened an ornate display cabinet and freed two hand-cut glasses from their golden glass cage. The slamming of the door mingled with a dull thud from the next room. She hurried back. The pizza delivery man was lying on the floor, lifeless, a piece of dough still stuck in his mouth.

Damn, it flashed through her mind. The pizza was meant for the dead woman. Who kills even the dead now? Shortly afterwards, she collapsed to the floor, pulled the soggy slice of pizza from the lifeless man's throat and, in rhythmic movements, forced her exhausted breath into the lifeless body.

During a brief pause, she reached for her mobile phone:

Roxanna here, send an ambulance immediately. And a hearse.

Then she placed her resuscitating hands on the man's breastbone again.

Let's see which car is faster, she muttered sarcastically. I should try a little harder. I think the pizza guy could get me a bit further.

When the two cars arrived, it was time for Roxanna to leave. On balance, the conversation with the dead woman had perhaps been less successful than expected, but she had still gained more useful information than she would have from an elaborate interrogation of all the neighbors within a kilometer radius.

She returned to the room once more to take a last look at the dead woman. What bureaucratic madness. The hearse she had called, and which arrived first was only allowed to take one person, the pizza delivery man. The woman wasn't picked up for another hour and a half.

I'm sorry you have to wait, she said to the dead woman. Look on the bright side. An extra hour in her little palace instead of the cramped cooler. By the way, I'll do my best. You won't benefit from it anymore, but I'll do my best.

Then she left the dead woman. First, she would go to Harry's bar, she had been denied a nice pizza, and her stomach was rumbling. Harry's bar had the best smoky salad in the whole city, tomatoes stewed in nicotine, the artichokes coated in a thin layer of alcohol, the mussels with a hint of sweat from the more than 100 guests. She had never seen less than 100 chattering, nattering heads populate the dive.

Hi Roxie, it's the grey tomatoes again?

Roxanna nodded towards the landlord, two meters of manhood wide enough to fill any doorway. In his hands, the glasses were nothing more than thimbles, the plates small porcelain chips at best.

Let me guess, Harry said. Four is too high, two maybe. No, two is too low. Three, I bet you got three more murders today.

A whole one and a half, Roxanna shook her head. A woman who's dead as a doornail – she couldn't help but think of the little grey mouse that sometimes scurried around her old flat – and a pizza delivery man on his way to the hospital in a hearse. Quite off today, Harry.

The landlord agreed with her.

Not my day either. However, the salad's free. But you'll have a drink, won't you? I have to live on something too.

Not from my liver, Roxanna laughed. The dead woman bought me three whiskies. Harry, that's enough for today.

A gaunt figure was crouching in the far corner of the bar. Narrow as a board, folded up like a penknife, a greasy hat pulled far down over his face. Roxanna noticed the stranger immediately. She had never seen him before. Her instinct told her that there was something to get from him. She bent forward imperceptibly.

Hey Harry, that bloke back there. Do you know anything about him?

A madman, Harry replied. Not been here long. But every day from morning till night. Always a pile of books on the table. Papal history. Reads everything about the popes from morning till night. Well, I don't care, the main thing is that he eats and drinks plenty.

Believe it or not, he really does. Breakfast, lunch, coffee, snacks. If he's not reading, he's eating. You wouldn't believe it if you saw him.

Roxanna nodded.

I'll sit with him. There's no free seat anyway.

That's all right, Harry replied. But make sure he doesn't eat your salad. I can't guarantee anything.

The inspector disappeared. She staggered indifferently through the room, only stopping in front of the table in the far corner.

Excuse me, may I sit down? It's the last free seat.

The man addressed did not look up. His eyes continued to glide over the colorfully illustrated glossy pages of a thick book, littered with the fat bodies of red-robed papal figures.

Roxanna had already eaten half the salad when the stranger looked up for the first time.

What do you want? he asked abruptly. You're a policeman – sorry, a policewoman.

The inspector hesitated. She had obviously underestimated her interlocutor.

Bull's eye, she replied curtly. But don't worry, I'm not on duty.

That's when it's most dangerous, said the man.

He closed the book in a flash, put a banknote on the table and stood up.

You should try pizza. Those grey tomatoes. Order a pizza with salami and pepperoni. Onions extra.

With these words, the stranger jumped forward. Roxanna tried to trip him up, but to no avail. The lank figure had disappeared into the dusky evening.

Suddenly Harry appeared. He held a book out to Roxanna.

If you don't turn me in. A little pickpocket trick. I pulled it out of the guy's coat pocket when he left the room in a hurry. Maybe you could use it.

Harry, you're a treasure, Roxanna burst out.
And Harry was more than a treasure. In the book, used as a bookmark, was a woman's business card: Michelle Denatielle.

Nice address, Roxanna whispered.
It would be best if she paid the person a visit.

The flat extended over the entire floor. A lift had been installed on the outside of the building, facing the rear courtyard, especially for this flat. A security code had been installed in three places: at the beginning, to get the lift; another password to set the lift in motion after entering and a final one for upstairs, to open the lift door that led directly to the flat.

Of course, there was also a staircase. But it ended on the fourth floor. Bricked up, only accessible via a security door. A third, more theoretical access consisted of the spiral rescue staircase on the outside.

Michelle Denatielle had waged a long bureaucratic campaign to have this staircase demolished or at least relocated. In vain. In this case, bureaucracy did not stop at money. Some narrow-minded, conscientious official had channeled all his energy and satisfaction into denying the well-known Michelle Denatielle her request. Unfortunately, this petty war had been publicized by the press, so that even if it had been legal, the mayor could not alter the matter without immediately sinking miserably into a terrible suspicion of corruption.

If you would be so kind as to turn round, Michelle asked the stranger. You understand, because of security.

The stranger nodded and turned his gaunt face to the closed door.

It's no problem to get into my flat, said Michelle. The problem is getting out again.

The stranger didn't react.

You see, this is my life insurance, so to speak. Let's assume you were going to kill me when we got upstairs. Of course you're not going to. I have a feeling of that. Only theoretically, let's assume theoretically. You won't be able to get out of the flat on your own. Maybe you'll make it back into the lift. Maybe you'll manage to get the lift to go down. But you won't be able to open the door downstairs on your own. Only I can open the door for you from the flat. You see, if I were dead, who would do it? You would be trapped like in a cage, the police would only have to collect you.

The stranger still didn't react. He fixed his gaze on a small hand mirror, which he held facing backwards to watch the woman. A security measure, perhaps, but he didn't like turning his back on anyone. The front of the body was there for the pleasant side of life, the unpleasant usually crept up from behind, this was where the dark side of existence lay.

Is the price still the same? the stranger asked abruptly.

If the goods are right, yes. As discussed. You will be reimbursed for the expenses separately, in return for a receipt, of course. The rest, if everything is in order.

Five minutes later, Michelle Denatielle was sitting with the stranger at a huge marble table, carved out of a single stone, worked over endless hours by masterful hands to look original and old and yet function perfectly in a modern way.

The stranger opened his bag and carefully lifted out a leather-wrapped square object. He carefully placed his gift on the table. He reached into his pocket and placed a thick pack of bills and receipts on the stone slab. Then he reached into his jacket once more and when his hand reappeared, it was clutching a revolver.

I have nothing to hide, said the stranger matter-of-factly. But you will understand that I also need my security.

With these words, he placed the gun on the cold tabletop. Michelle barely noticed him. She had hastily begun to remove the item from the leather cloak.

Michelle was satisfied.

How much will it cost if you tell me how to do it myself next time?

The stranger looked at her in amazement. He was a professional, the best in his field. And this spoilt young woman, who had grown up in a swamp of money, wanted to top him.

Twice as much, he replied curtly.

Twice as much? Michelle started up in horror. Are you crazy?

The stranger remained calm.

You see, I'm losing my best customer. If you do it yourself, why do you still need me? I have to take precautions, without my best customer I really have to take precautions.

Michelle thought about it. Money didn't matter. But she didn't like getting involved in impertinence. And twice as much, wasn't it a bottomless impertinence?

Fine, she said briefly. Let's say double the price, if your explanations are plausible to me. You could tell me anything. If I believe you, you'll get twice as much, half immediately, the other half when I've done it myself according to your instructions.

The stranger nodded his head, barely visible. Stubborn thing, his interlocutor, he thought, and saw fit to place his hand briefly on the revolver.

Agreed, but always remember: I am a man who appreciates security.

Very noticeably, it would not have been necessary at all, he withdrew his hand and let it glide slowly over the revolver.

Neither of them spoke a word for the next half hour. The woman leafed attentively through the book the stranger had brought her. It showed imposing men, surrounded by red silk and purple, in the background an exuberant wealth of paintings, tapestries, masterpieces of craftsmanship dripping with gold, plump bodies, not always clothed.

What are you actually looking for?

It was the first time that the stranger had broken his policy of not asking a client why he wanted something. But the young woman was searching in the old book, so feverishly tense and at the same time enraptured, as if she were looking for something on which her existence depended. His words did not reach her, so he repeated the question.

I have taken the liberty of leafing through the book in advance. Tell me what you're looking for, maybe I can help you.

Only now did Michelle Denatielle look up. She fixed the stranger with a sharp gaze that penetrated his body faster than a revolver bullet.

Justice! You won't believe this, but I'm only looking for one tiny justice. Hard to find, buried under 500 years. But faith will move the mountain of 500 years.

It was time to part from the stranger. She had the book, and she now knew how to get more books herself, in case the right one was not yet in front of her.

Michelle stood up calmly, opened a desk drawer and pulled out a revolver. She pointed it at the stranger. Without a word, she pulled the trigger.

You see, I need security too, Michelle said as she looked into the other man's pale face.

He couldn't get a word out.

Forgive the little joke, Michelle burst out and put the unloaded revolver back in the drawer. At one point I thought you were going too far with your demands. And then you asked why. Who did you train with? You don't ask questions like that.

Excuse me, the stranger murmured, slowly regaining his speech. I was fascinated by the way you searched through the book. I've never seen anyone go after something like that.

Michelle looked at the stranger. He was certainly no looker, no dress man from a fashion catalogue, but at least he was average.

I'll explain it to you, she said, placing her hand on him. A long story, 500 years old, it takes time to explain 500 years.

She straightened up and pulled the man over onto the bed, hanging on to his arm she let herself fall backwards and flung her shoes across the room as she fell. With just a few movements, she was lying there undressed and before the stranger knew it, she had peeled him out of his clothes too. Not a bad decision, the woman thought, because behind the somewhat old-fashioned clothes was a perfectly acceptable, above-average content.

It must have been 500 years ago, she began. Rome, summer, lots of sunshine, a huge building in the center. The air was buzzing in the midday heat, people dragged themselves sluggishly through the city, poorly dressed, wrapped in thick robes, despite the heat.

She continued her story in an even tone, realizing as she spoke that the stranger was now lying on top of her, the face of his slim body weighing more heavily on her with each passing moment.

It was 1.35 am when a drunk man wandering through the town stumbled across the dead man by chance. Less than ten minutes later, the gendarmerie had arrived with a deafening noise and the wailing sires had startled the residents out of their sleep. As luck would have it, Roxanna arrived at the scene of the incident at almost the same time. She had come from Harry's bar, which was not far away. It was her territory anyway, so she would have the case on her hands by tomorrow at the latest. After a brief consultation with the local gendarme in charge, she decided to start the investigation immediately. Despite the three whiskies at the first crime scene and the encores in Harry's bar.

Half an hour later, she was sitting in Michelle Denatielle's flat. She couldn't quite remember how she had got in there. In any case, she suddenly found herself in one of the largest flats in the city; all the flats she had ever lived in added up to only a fraction of the area of this flat.

Roxanna was in a bad mood. What a trivial murder mystery she had got herself into. Three dead bodies, or to be more precise two dead bodies, evenly split in terms of equality, a man and a woman, and a pizza delivery man hovering between the hospital and the morgue. Three dead bodies, what a cheap murder mystery, the good ones got by with one and the best ones she'd read didn't need a single one.

Never mind, she thought, it always hit the wrong person anyway. The dead man must obviously have been in this flat. The reconstructed height of the fall allowed no other conclusion.

Damn it all, why had he fled from Harry's bar and was now lying shattered on the polished cobblestones in one of the best residential areas in the city? Was there a connection between the dead people? This Michelle Denatielle, what role did she play?

There's no need to reproduce the conversation. Both women were marked by fatigue. Their senses slightly dulled by alcohol, a meaningless, awkward conversation ensued. In the meantime, Roxanna had learnt more about the dead man through a call from the police headquarters. A small-time crook, but one who specialized in stealing art objects on demand from the most unusual places in the world. What made him special were the unusual places where he worked. Mostly antiquated, not particularly well-guarded libraries.

And you say he threatened you with this revolver? Michelle nodded.

I own a gun myself, with a license of course. For security reasons. Suddenly he was standing in my flat. Don't ask me how he got in. I've been fighting a petty official for years to have the fire escape taken down. The whole house is mine. Most of the time I live alone. I'd rather burn to death than live in constant fear of some-one breaking in via the fire escape.

Michelle smiled. Only now did it occur to her that she would use the incident, as a kind of pleasant spin-off, to enforce the demolition of the outside staircase. By now at the latest, this stuffy official would no longer be able to put forward any useful counterarguments.

And then, Roxanna asked, tell me what happened after that.

He was obviously looking for a particular object. Well, look around, I have a few things to offer. Basically, a beginner. At least that's what I felt. I let myself be unobtrusively pushed back to the desk and pulled my pistol out of the drawer. It's always open at night so I can get to it more quickly in an emergency. All I could see was him dropping his gun, totally perplexed, and rushing to the door behind which the lift was located.

I understand that, but why on earth do you have a lift with a lift-up floor?

For safety's sake. I have a special license – two to be precise, one from the prefect of police and one from the building authority. It cost me a lot of paperwork. If someone attacks me and, in the worst case, takes me to the afterlife, they should at least have the pleasure of finding their way out through a bottomless lift. Saves the justice system and the taxpayer a lot of money. Fortunately, we're not in America, where they have to make security arrangements for crooks so they can't hurt themselves breaking in. But I can reassure you. I'll find out if he has a family and give the surviving dependents an adequate settlement.

Michelle thought about the agreed sum. Originally, she wanted to burn the money. The stranger had earned it, she wanted to remain fair, albeit within certain limits. The idea of giving the money to the bereaved had just occurred to her and it would ease her conscience. With the money, the woman could find somebody else. Who would want to live with a crook?

It makes sense to me, Roxanna interrupted. I don't think I need to ask any more questions. How do I find the way out?

Michelle pointed to the lift.

Don't worry, the floor panel is firmly locked again, as it should be for decent visitors. Although – policemen are not among my favorite guests.

I can understand that. I prefer to see my colleagues only when they're on duty.

As she turned round, she noticed a somewhat strange but distinctive odor. Had they been having an affair?

She made a quick note. The coroner would have to pay attention to a particular part of the shattered body. After all, these coroners were all slobs. If they didn't poke their noses into traces of secretion, all the victims were nothing more than the result of an unfortunate chain of circumstances.

When Roxanna stepped out onto the street again, they had already picked up the dead man. Too bad, she thought, the time was far advanced. But she would have liked to have had a little chat with the victim, even if it was night, even in the middle of the street. After all, there were three strange incidents with fatal outcomes to clear up, so what did she care about the irritated looks of any passers-by if she had spoken to the victim under these circumstances. But the dead man had already left, and she really didn't want to drive to the morgue after him. Maybe to-morrow, she would see. Although there was proba-bly no point in going tomorrow, as time went on the dead didn't exactly become more talkative.

The following day, the dignitary woke up when the sun had already completed part of its morning round. Over the years, his servant had developed a keen sense of when he would wake up the next morning. Actually, it had less to do with intuition than with math and a little logic. The servant simply paid attention to how long the noises from the bed-chamber lasted, totaled up the usual time of night-time restorative sleep and in this way knew quite precisely when to bring breakfast to his bed.

An unpardonable omission, the dignitary woke up without finding the usual delicacies by his bedside. It was almost as disastrous when the food had been sitting next to the bed for too long and some of its freshness had dissolved in the musty room.

Satisfied, the dignitary reached for the food. He was no fool. His alert eyes had long since realized that the servant was taking advantage of unobserved moments to watch the naked female body through the precious telescope. His eyes had long since dis-covered that on the south wall of the room, incon-spicuously next to a magnificent tapestry, there was a hole in the brickwork through which he could ob-serve what was happening in the bedchamber at any time. In a way, he was honored that a young servant had found his activities worthy enough of this un-heard-of risk in his old age. His vanity blinded him to the idea that the servant might be interested in any-thing other than the woman he regularly brought in.

All these trivial offences were pardonable, provided breakfast was served in bed at the right time the next morning. In his old age, the dignitary appreciated this, as it gave him sufficient strength for the coming day after a good night's sleep.

After the meal, the dignitary called the servant. Without a word, the servant cleared away the leftovers. He was about to leave when the patron stopped him.

Were you satisfied?

The servant blushed. He clumsily tried to hide his confusion behind indifference.

I don't understand you, Your Honor.

Well, replied the patron, perhaps I should give you a hand. I ordered the woman to be taken back to her hut at night.

I did so, Your Honor.

It should happen without detours.

What do you mean by that? Sometimes I have to take a different route to avoid meeting anyone.

And fate or chance always wants the route to go via your room?

The servant remained silent. Sinking into denial was of little help. Obviously, the dignitary knew much of what lay dormant in his mind as a dark secret.

Be patient, said the dignitary. Everything has its time. At some point, perhaps soon, my body will tire of the woman. If fate favors you before then, I will soon be afflicted with a stroke. Two ways, as you can see, to legitimately get what you desire. Just remember, I detest it when someone wallows in my chosen secretions. A disgusting thought for me. I advise you to be sensible. You are young. You have two cards in your hand: my weariness and my age. Are there higher trumps?

Michelle Denatielle searched in vain in the book for the last key to the puzzle in front of her. The effort had not necessarily been in vain, at least she now knew how to get hold of the books. She also had the names of two or three other men who offered similar services to the stranger's. But it was pointless to approach these men. Word had long since spread that one of their own had died in a strange way. No one could blame the woman for anything, let alone prove it. Even Inspector Roxanna could find no reasonable reason to doubt her innocence. Nevertheless, it would be pointless to approach another contact on the list. They sensed too great a risk to health and even life.

Based on these considerations, the woman decided to carry out the next action herself.

A week later, she was on a plane to Rome. The summer was still raging through Europe, the leaves hung scorched on the trees, trade winds drove clouds of dust through the streets of the parched cities. The people had taken refuge behind a pitiful hollow in the stone walls. They only came out of their dwellings in the evening, suspiciously peering around to see if the world still existed or if everything had long since been burnt up in a predicted apocalyptic firestorm.

Michelle had difficulty getting an air-conditioned taxi. She stood in the blistering heat for ten minutes before a limousine with a taxi sign came past. Behind the wheel was a young woman, presumably a student working to pay for her studies.

To the Vatican, Michelle said as she got in.

So, to the Vatican, repeated the young driver. Should I deliver you directly to the Pope?
Michelle shook her head, bored.

Do you know your way around the city? I mean, are you from Rome and not Milan or Florence?

A Roman for centuries, replied the young woman. We can trace our lineage back 500 years. All pretty and good Romans.
Michelle looked at the other woman. She had an even, finely drawn face, which she carried proudly facing forwards. Her body was slim and flat, interrupted at the top by two well-formed breasts, which were vaguely visible under her T-shirt. The upper part of her legs was covered by a mini dress.
Why hadn't she been born a man? she thought silently. For every ten beautiful women, there was at most one equally good-looking man.

Take me to the best hotel within a radius of 500 meters. Let's say 300 meters. Find me the best hotel that is no more than 300 meters from the Vatican.
The young woman was taken aback.

The Vatican is big, she replied. Which point of the Vatican do you mean?

You'll get it right, Michelle replied. Just get going. But make an effort, you won't regret it.

The hotel was within sight of the Vatican. On the first morning, Michelle Denatielle realized that she had to get up early to join the kilometer-long queue of people waiting to enter the papal chambers. She let two more days pass in indifference. She used the time to visit some of the sights in the venerable city center. In the evening light of the setting sun, she climbed to the highest tier of the Colosseum and gazed at the center of the arena from a distant height. In her imagination, the exposed dark pits awoke and spewed out armed heroes, ready to fight to the death with trained beasts. She thought she could hear the sound of a nearby sea in the balmy evening breeze, the Tiber gushing into the theatre, turning it into a churning lake on which galleys of men clashed.

On the opposite stand, she clearly recognized the ecclesiastical dignitaries, escaped from their time, applauding the fighters vigorously. When she became aware of the venerable figures, she realized again the reason for her stay.

Next day she would carry out her plan.

She closed her eyes and replayed the stranger's statements in her memory. His face appeared. So did his body, which fell unclothed from the top tier of the battle arena, skillfully dodging gladiatorial fighters and disappearing with a dull thud into the open hatch of a lift that had suddenly appeared in the confusion of fighters, predators and galleys as a menetekel of modern times.

She repeated the most important points of her plan over and over again until she had mastered everything like a somnambulist. Satisfied, she opened her eyes. She stared ahead in disbelief, trying to separate thought from reality, because suddenly a young woman stood in front of her. She had moved her legs slightly apart to give herself a secure footing. It looked as if she was expecting an attack. A few seconds passed before Michelle's eyes adjusted from the darkness of the introspective gaze to the dazzling light of the setting sun.

Now she recognized the woman. It was the taxi-driving student who had chauffeured her from the airport to the hotel. Coincidence? There were no coincidences, at least not for Michelle Denatielle. Nevertheless, she put on a harmless face to find out the reason for the other woman's appearance.

Her caution bade her to hide her recognition. Seemingly indifferent, she took a few steps forward, rounding a tight bend to avoid the other woman. Just as the woman began to disappear from her field of vision, she felt a hand grab her sleeve and yank her around forcefully.

Why are you pretending? the young woman asked.

Michelle reflected. Her mask of cluelessness, should she let it slip, let it fall to the floor?

I don't know what you want from me.

It doesn't matter, replied the other. You'll find out. Very soon. By the way, my name is Alessia. My surname doesn't matter. I change it like a dress. But I've got used to Alessia. What does that name sound like? I've often asked myself. My favorite interpretation is this: everything, si, aha. When I want something, I want everything, you know? Don't ask me how many names I tried out before I came up with Alessia. Call me Alessia. I like it when my partners call me that.

Partners? Michelle repeated. I can hardly imagine what we could do together.

You don't need your imagination, let's say not for that. I think you'll find out soon enough. By the way, have you had your fill of these old moldy, blood-soaked stones?

For now, I suppose, Michelle replied. You will probably have discovered that I have a fondness for old walls.

Alessia nodded.

If they're full of books, si? Let's go to a café. On the other side of the road, we have to go up the hill. But it's worth it. From the top, Rome lies at your feet.

It's rare for a city to lay itself at the feet of a woman, mocked Michelle. Do I have a chance of rejecting your proposal?

We live in a free country, replied Alessia. You see, freedom consists of being able to feel that you are free to choose, even though you know, well, I'm sure you understand what I'm saying.

Michelle understood. Wordlessly, she ran off, descending the steep steps into time-worn history, while the oddly familiar stranger followed her.

It had become much cooler by now. Michelle wished she was wearing a fluffy jumper. Instead, her upper body was only covered by a strapless T-shirt. The unprotected areas of her skin were turning into a goose bump landscape of swelling mini craters.

Rome is a desert, said Alessia, sipping her cappuccino. You still have a lot to learn. Have you ever been to the desert?

Michelle nodded. Obviously, the other girl knew more about her than she could possibly imagine.

I travelled around the world for two years, Michelle replied. For the sole purpose of setting foot on every country in the world. Not so easy. Every moment I thought that another revolution somewhere in the world could give birth to a new country. After my first trip, I had to take six months to visit all the countries that had emerged in the meantime.

You've visited everything, interrupted Alessia, except the Vatican. Why?

It's like eating with ordinary people. A small bite, the best one, they save it for last.

Alessia agreed with her.

And sometimes, unexpectedly, the dear relatives come by and snatch it from under their noses.

That may be. I hardly have any relatives.

At first, I wondered how you did it with Alessandro. Falling out of a lift. Maybe the police will believe you.

Michelle wanted to say something, but Alessia continued unperturbed.

I was only interested at first. Alessandro meant too little to me. Now it's only of interest to me because...

You don't mean that, do you? Michelle interjected.

Let's drop the subject, said Alessia. The money was a noble gesture. Here in Italy, we appreciate a sense of family.

He had earned the money, Michelle replied coolly. Since we're in the middle of a quiz, I'd also like to ask a small question.

Alessia looked at her.

Ask, I'm always in favor of openness.

How did you manage to catch me in a taxi at the airport?

Alessia thought about it. Minutes passed. The cappuccino was still steaming. At the neighboring table, a well-to-do gentleman was making out with a streetwalker. Evening birds were nesting in the cypress trees and singing about the setting sun.

Finally, she looked at Michelle.

It wasn't difficult. Not worth telling you either. But take it as a little reminder that I'm good for surprises.

This Alessandro, were you friends?

Alessia fell silent again for a few seconds.

Yes, but not in the way you think. We were business partners. Rome is divided. It's always been divided. We both owned the papal library.

Suddenly they were right in the middle of business. Michelle was surprised at the other's sudden openness. She obviously loved surprises. And a straight path is sometimes a surprise, especially when you're walking over dangerous cliffs.

Did you really think we'd get you the right book the first time? Alessia laughed. We would have milked you for a while. Be honest. You wouldn't have done it any differently. That's why the milking continues. I will continue alone. I'll put my hands on your udders alone.

The mood changed at these words. There was a lot contained in that sentence: an intention, a threat, blackmail – or a declaration of love?

Michelle stood up.

I told you about my travels. I've seen every country. Not just to set foot in it. Amazonia disgusted me. That stuffy, humid air, the sweat-soaked clothes constantly clinging to your skin. Annoying blowflies are constantly circling around you, mistaking you for a living carcass.

Alessia remained silent, so Michelle continued.

You know my hotel. Come round when you've come to your senses. I'll let you talk to me about almost anything.

With these words, she turned round and disappeared from the café-laden scene into the dawning darkness of the awakening city.

The dignitary possessed clairvoyant abilities. People didn't care where these powers came from; in their dreary everyday lives, all that mattered was the fact that they were extraordinary. Within four weeks, he had suffered his first minor stroke. His speech had remained intact, both arms could be lifted with the appropriate caution of old age and his legs were still able to carry his stocky body through existence. Only a few muscles around a central point of his body failed to function.

Centuries later, this unusual pinpoint accuracy would have given rise to sensationalized medical speculation. After a further orbit of the moon, another, larger stroke had surgically divided the dignitary's body exactly into two halves, a right one, wasting away lifelessly, and a left one, frantically trying to snatch the lost functions from the swamp of oblivion. Even the center of the body was slightly altered by the new stroke. In rare moments, one half of this central structure would tense up and bend into bizarre figurations, without gaining any function from the bizarre shapes.

As his physical abilities diminished, the dignitary turned more and more to his eyes, which had lost none of their power and continued to scrutinize life with a suspicious gaze. As he looked, he remembered the precious tapestry on the wall and the dormant black hole set into the wall next to it.

One day he had the idea of hiding an absurd confusion behind the masquerade of his illness. That day, he put on a confusing play for those around him, which culminated in an order to take the naked woman from the hut to the palace and employ her as a servant in his chambers from then on. Nobody knew how to interpret this request, but as the doctors had strictly forbidden any excitement, they granted him his wish, still believing that it had arisen from a confused part of his brain.

From that day on, the image of the naked woman's body adorned the chambers. The servants pretended not to notice all these grotesque events and tried to flee in dignified apathy every time the naked woman appeared.

Only the dignitary's eyes rested on the woman's figure at every opportunity and watched the woman's various activities every day, always catching new glimpses of the female nude.

Many moons passed through the land in this simple-minded way, autumn shook the trees bare, and the approaching winter ate into the walls of the houses with damp cold. The woman, despite her unrivalled regular beauty, had become confused in one part of her head years ago and refused to put on clothes despite the cold.

Thus, the rooms were heated daily by hissing fires, whose warmth made the past summer seem like a cool breeze. Whimsical thoughts grew in the dignitary's head in the winter heat, while the naked female body gave rise to old desires with each passing day. The two merged into a dangerous symbiosis that was heading towards a fateful moment.

On the afternoon of the eleventh day of a wintry month, 500 years ago, the dignitary lay on his bed. The naked woman climbed on to chairs and tables, stripping the walls of cobwebs. The dignitary's eyes crawled up the slender legs from her feet, which stretched tirelessly as she worked, ending in the elliptical halves of her buttocks.

What are you doing there? stammered the dignitary.

The woman looked at him. They were the first words he had spoken in months.

Leave the work.

The dignitary beckoned the woman to him. He grabbed her naked body and pulled her down onto the bed. The woman had indifferent memories of moments long past. The dignitary laboriously turned his heavy body on its side and lowered his massive weight onto the woman. Then he rolled his massive body completely onto the slender body. The woman tried to push the excessive weight up, but in vain. She struggled to catch her breath, the air between both of their faces was laboring to find its way.

Suddenly, the dignitary turned his head to the side and placed his fleshy cheeks on the woman's nose and mouth. The woman's breath turned to gasps, the blue of her eyes spread across the fine features of her face, her feet convulsing into unnatural positions. The dignitary looked up, his eyes searching the tapestry and the black hole resting beside it. He clearly recognized the servant's eye in the black air and his features, resting on the woman, mutated into the grand pose of an odious victor.

Roxanna sat at her old desk, tirelessly hammering away at the laptop. In the other corner of the office was her aide, Sergeant Henry. Years ago, the indifference of his will had left him on a middle rung of the career ladder, from which he could easily meet all the financial demands that life placed on him. It had been three years since this willful Roxanna had been put in front of him. He had got used to that too and was just waiting to retire in a year's time. The drone of the keys was torturing his head.

Take your frustration out somewhere else, Sergeant Henry blurted out.

Roxanna looked up.

All right. We'll swap. Half the report is done. You'll stroke the other half into the computer with your delicate hands.

Own goal, thought Sergeant Henry, biting his lips. I don't want to diminish your earnings, Roxanna. My pension is safe. Who knows what it will be like for you.

He added with a smile: I think it will be more favorable for you if you finish writing yourself. Did you mention that you went back to the morgue because you still had a few questions for the dead Madame Richaud?

Roxanna remained silent and the sergeant continued.

You see, age makes us correct people. I wouldn't find a plausible explanation for not mentioning that in the report. The prefect has a mania about completeness. You should be aware of it.

That's all right, Roxanna groaned at the covert little blackmail. But don't forget that I have the memory of an elephant.

Tell me, Roxanna, how did you come up with Madame Richaud's murderer? I mean, the pizza delivery man doesn't kill the woman first only to poison himself afterwards.

Love tragedy and greed, Roxanna replied. The two of them were having an affair, she quickly discovered. Then the usual. Another woman. Well, the pizza delivery man, this Henry – Roxanna smiled, I hope the similarity of names doesn't mean anything – this Henry decides to get rid of Madame Richaud. He's got someone else and besides, she's left him five per cent of her fortune in her will.

Five per cent, not much for bed services, Sergeant Henry murmured.

You don't know the amount of this Madame Richaud's fortune!

Sergeant Henry shook his head.

I'm sure you'll tell me next.

10 million, Roxanna replied. 5 per cent of her fortune equals 10 million. Do the math yourself. All in all, 200 million in property.

Sergeant Henry whistled through his teeth.

Why do I always end up with the wrong people? A woman who leaves me 10 million. You don't find that every day.

You're not handsome enough, mocked Roxanna. For 10 million, a woman can afford a good man. Everything has to be just right: 1.85 meters tall, blonde hair, deep blue eyes, broad shoulders and a narrow waist, and what do you call it today: a cute ass. Look at yourself in the mirror, you'd have to pay the same price for a woman to take you.

Sergeant Henry was seething, but Roxanna wasn't fazed and even went one better.

I'm only talking about the cover. Then there's the content: self-assured, witty, charming, funny, courteous, a touch crazy, sporty: tennis, skiing, horse riding, all minimum requirements – not forgetting culture, just as well versed in classical opera as upmarket disco.

Such a man exists? Sergeant Henry interrupted.

Roxanna nodded.

The pizza delivery man had everything. Don't ask me why he was delivering pizzas with those genetics.

What made you think he killed Madame Richaud?

I told you about his lover. Typical constellation, like in any bad thriller. Suddenly someone else turns up, not rich, not a magnificent villa in the best residential neighborhood in Paris, just enchanting, enchantingly beautiful, enchanting in character and beauty. Our pizza delivery man was helplessly in love. But there was a problem.

I can guess. He began to enjoy the sweet life. So, he killed Madame Richaud. The will would have opened every gate in the world to him. Only, continued Sergeant Henry, why did he come back with a poisoned pizza? Why this Snow-White performance?

It's a good thing you're retiring soon, Roxanna teased. You could stay in the force for another hundred years without solving a more complicated case. Why does a perpetrator shoot himself in the leg? Certainly not because he's a masochist.

Sergeant Henry shook his head.

That pizza delivery man didn't shoot himself in the leg.

Did you ever understand the word analogy? He had poisoned the pizza. Two halves. One heavily dosed, the other with only a little poison.

I see, our Snow White apple.

Roxanna nodded.

In his agitation, he took a bite from the wrong side.

Now you just have to explain to me why he came back. Madame Richaud was already dead, he had killed her before, according to you.

Psychopath, Roxanna explained, wanted to be sure she was really dead. Some murderers kill their victims twice.

She laughed out loud. Maybe that was the reason.

But now seriously. It was staged. A theatre performance for the police.

What punishment awaits him? Sergeant Henry asked.

None, replied Roxanna, or the maximum penalty. He's already been convicted. The hospital called this morning. Our pizza delivery boy didn't survive his poisoning.

All that's missing is the seven dwarves to shake him awake.

Let's drop it, said Roxanna and started hammering away at the laptop again. Story time is over. I've got work to do.

For some reason, Sergeant Henry kept staring at her. Annoyed, Roxanna looked up.

I know you still want an explanation of what the fatal lift accident in the fifth arrondissement is all about. We have checked everything. Every detail meticulously researched. This Michelle Denatielle is absolutely clean. It was a tragic accident, the occupational hazard of a burglar. I didn't understand what this Alessandro was doing with Michelle Denatielle of all people, but never mind, a reasonable little secret. Do you know what he specialized in? Stealing books. Not just any books. Commissioned orders, with the necessary cash they could order any book from the Vatican's papal library from him. But this Michelle Denatielle is not the type for old, venerable books. No matter. Maybe our Alessandro wanted to switch. In any case, the case is closed for me.

Sergeant Henry clapped his hands in approval.

Three deaths solved in one week. Even if I hate to do it, I have to pay you a big compliment.

Roxanna stopped listening. She was busy hammering her report into the laptop again. Sergeant Henry didn't notice that she strangely left huge gaps in some places.

Roxanna was at an age when it was starting to become questionable to cavort on the beach in a skimpy bikini. She compensated for her age with the fitness of a well-trained body that could hide behind many a decathlete. Lost in thought, she lay on the warm sand and let the heated white grains of sand roll over her skin.

She had well and truly earned a week in the Caribbean, even if it was only an all-inclusive holiday. Age had turned Sergeant Henry into a gossiping washerwoman. Her explanation made sense to him and, as he sometimes didn't exactly move in the most respectable circles, he would publicize that the case had been closed. Whether it was any help, she couldn't say, but it gave her peace of mind from Sergeant Henry for the time being.

She tried again and again to put the pieces of the puzzle together. In vain. She couldn't even begin to recognize a coherent picture. Young women with long bare legs walked past her, happy chuckling mingling with the monotonous sound of the waves. Less than ten meters away from her lay a man in his mid-forties, most parts of his body already nicely tanned. Someone should switch off the cooker, Roxanna thought. Instead, a prankster had rammed a sign into the floor next to the sleeping man.

Gone for a moment – please turn in 20 minutes.

Roxanna would have liked to lay her head on the sun-tanned man's arm a few times, not because of the man, he didn't attract her, she just had the feeling that it was part of the aloof ease of the beach idyll. For lack of opportunity, she went over her previous investigation results again and again. She couldn't help feeling that all three deaths were linked together as if by an iron chain. Where was the connecting link? What did the pizza delivery man have to do with Alessandro, the book thief? Was there a connection between Madame Richaud and Alessandro, or even between Madame Richaud and this Michelle Denatielle?

She could twist it, she could turn it round and round, as often as she liked, but she couldn't come up with a viable explanation. But wasn't it strange? The names of three dead people kept running through her head and the image of Michelle Denatielle kept popping up. She must hold the key to everything. Next week, right after her short holiday, she would visit the grave of the dead Madame Richaud. Her ghost had to be floating around somewhere, why not in the cemetery? She still had a few questions for the dead woman, perhaps she would get the inspiration there to find out how everything was connected.

Otherwise, she would take a sword and simply cut through the tangle of intertwined possible connections. Perhaps there was a small hidden truth inside this tangle that held everything together invisibly. This random blow with a sword, it didn't have to be targeted. Something devious, something senseless, something that set the sticky mush of interwoven events in motion again. An exhumation, for example. She would request an exhumation; no one had yet investigated whether the poison in the pizza that had killed the messenger could also be found in Alessandro, the book thief.

Interesting perspective, thought Roxanna, then one and the same culprit would have Madame Richaud, the pizza delivery man and Alessandro on his conscience, which meant nothing other than that the pizza delivery man…

When she looked up, the tanned man in his forties stood up next to her. He stretched his ageing body, revealing wrinkles that had previously been hidden by fat bulges. The exposed wrinkles stood out bizarrely against the rest of his body in an insignificant white color.

Not done yet, thought Roxanna, shuddering a little at the thought of having had the feeling of resting her head on a sleeping body just a few minutes ago.

Are you sure that Signora Denatiel e has left?

Absolutely, replied the porter. Three days ago. She seemed to be in a great hurry. Urgent family matters, if I remember correctly.

Alessia stamped her feet on the floor. That nasty little toad. She wasn't getting off that easily.

The porter noticed the woman's agitation and leant forward.

I might be able to think of something else. My age, signorina. There are good memory pills. But expensive, I tell you, very expensive.

Alessia understood. She opened her handbag, reached into her wallet and pulled out a 100 euro note. With a practiced grip, the porter let the money disappear into his pocket.

Expensive pills, signorina, very expersive memory pills. I can only buy pills for one half of my brain with 100 euros. You see, I have two. How am I supposed to know which half contains my memory?

Alessia looked at him searchingly. What the hell, she'd made that mistake. Alessandro had never been her cup of tea. But she was in his debt and the least she could do was to transfer him personally from Paris to Verona.

Unfortunately, she had thought that she could leave this Michelle unobserved for three days. A misjudgment. It couldn't be helped. At best, with the porter's knowledge. Reluctantly, she reached into her wallet again and this time took out a 200 euro note.

Who knows, maybe this porter had three halves of a brain.

The man grinned at the sight of the note and let it disappear into his jacket pocket just as inconspicuously as the first one. Then he reached into the front pocket of his jacket and pulled out a piece of paper.

Make a note of the address, he said curtly. I need the note back. The signora was waiting for a man. Every day. He never turned up. Then she left and gave me the note in case your visitor turned up.

Did she describe the man to you? Alessia asked excitedly.

The porter shook his head.

Only that he would ask about her, about the French woman with the Vatican book.

Alessia took a deep breath. This Michelle had tricked her. But she had rejoiced too soon. She looked at the note and smiled. Michelle Denatielle was now in Sydney. She would pay her a nice visit. She had always wanted to go to Sydney. Alessia copied down the address and slid the note back over the counter. Without a word, she turned round and left the hotel. The porter grinned and picked up the phone. He had earned 300 euros on the side. Not a bad start to the day.

A woman's voice answered on the other end.

She was there, said the porter, everything exactly as you said.

Excellent, the female voice breathed back. You already have 1000 euros. You'll get the other 1000 euros tomorrow.

The porter breathed a sigh of satisfaction. The woman on the other end of the phone was also relieved. She was thinking of her grandmother. Grandma swore that the best place to hide sweets was an open spot on the dining table. People like to search, she always said. Nobody searches where something jumps right into their eyes. Alessia would search anywhere in the world, but not in the open place on the dining table.

With a gracious movement of his left arm, the dignitary beckoned the servant over. His massive body was lying next to the naked woman again, the dignitary's eyes fixed on a mirror mounted at an angle on the ceiling. The lifeless image of the naked woman had floated up into the air and remained on the mirror. Plump baroque figures framed the scene and gazed wide-eyed at the woman's figure. The servant had approached submissively and remained silent beside the bed. His master did not notice him, his old eyes remained fixed on the image of the naked woman floating on the ceiling.

At last he noticed the servant. His mouth opened sluggishly, his tongue pushed restlessly against his wrinkled lips, trying to mold the escaping air into words.

You, you can have her, the dignitary groaned.

He grabbed his paralyzed arm with his left hand, pulled it up and let it fall onto the woman's buttocks one last time. A dull, lifeless sound travelled between the two dead figures and echoed in the room. Mechanically, the servant lifted his master's dead arm, which had clawed into the flesh in rhythmic convulsions. He released the cramped fingers from the cold fleshy buttocks and slid both his arms under the woman. Gingerly he lifted the beauty-clad figure into the stuffy air of the room, He walked reverently across the soft carpets, marveling at the centuries-old faces on the walls.

The path led him to his chamber, where he laid the lifeless body of the woman on his bed. His hand ran over the delicate face and caressed the thin lips. Only now did he realize that the woman was naked, although he had been aware of it again and again, and felt the inappropriateness of this state at such a moment. He hurried into his master's chambers, opened an oak wardrobe and took out a silk festive gown for the special holidays. He wrapped the woman's naked body in it and laid her to rest for the night.

Two hours later, the lamps in the dignitary's bedchamber had gone out. His eyes found no rest, trying to penetrate the dark room to see if the image of the woman was still floating on the ceiling. Only a silent shadow fell from the night mirror. It floated over the soft floor carpet without a sound. The dignitary's paralyzed right arm jerked restlessly and clung tightly to the edge of the bed.

He heard soft footsteps from the foot of the bed, the rhythm of their gait seemed familiar to him, but they did not respond to his speech. Two hands made their way to one of the bedposts and knotted a finger-thick cord to the wooden post. In the darkness, the other end of the rope began to move, snaking over the linen sheet and crawling across the dignitary's body. He felt the cool, scaly skin of the creature as it slowly snaked over his legs. Tensely, he clenched his healthy left hand to ward off an attack. But the snake-like creature sensed the lurking hand and dodged onto the paralyzed arm hanging down. Despite the paralysis, the skin of the crippled part of the body registered the trembling vibration of the creature.

The dignitary waited until it had approached within reach of his left hand. The lifeless woman's face lit up in the darkness to show the black serpentine figure the way. In the glow of the sudden brightness, the dignitary recognized the form of the hostile creature. His distorted mouth opened to let out a rattling cry for help. At the same moment, the black serpent thrust forward like an arrow, disappearing into the dignitary's open jaws and sinking its teeth into the old flesh.

The man's open mouth collapsed in a flash and the rows of teeth crashed together with shattering force, separating the black creature's firmly bitten head from its rope-like body. The effect of the poison had already set in, the distorted mouth tried in vain to pull the rows of teeth apart again, to let new air flow into the struggling body. Slowly, the gasping breath died away. A dark blueness spread over the body and merged with the black night.

Two hands slid over the dignitary's cold face. With a practiced grip, they pulled the mouth apart and fingered the severed head out of the dead man's throat. Then they unknotted the rope from the wooden post and dissolved into the darkness of the night.

After a week in the Caribbean, Roxanna had acquired more color than during the entire summer.

In a good mood, she returned to Paris, where people were preparing for the approaching rigidity of winter in the grey desolation of autumn.

The holiday had not helped her solve the case. However, she was well rested, which seemed to her to be a favorable prerequisite for further work, and she approached the case unencumbered by any previous considerations, as if it had just been assigned to her. First, she paid a visit to Madame Richaud. In a way, this was the only new unencumbered decision she had made, as she had been thinking about it for a long time. Few people spent their time in the central cemetery during the inhospitable weather. Roxanna, in her rested tan, looked like a provocative foreign body that disturbed the pale mourning of the cemetery visitors.

Here, people wore a distinguished grey pallor on their faces, which also had to be a little puffy at best due to welling tears. Roxanna's smooth brown Caribbean skin color was a disturbing reminder that she had found her way back to a pleasurable life through the death of another.

The inspector was not fazed. She knew her way around cemeteries. In summer, her walks didn't take her through the parks of Paris, but across the spruced-up burial grounds, and if her flat mates hadn't found it repulsive, she would have moved her jogs from the banks of the Seine to the cemeteries.

Roxanna stood in front of the grave and let the words of the inscription sink in.

Rest in peace – what an ordinary, meaningless text. How could someone rest in peace in a rotting wooden box, two meters deep in damp, cold earth? Involuntarily, the image of the deceased appeared in her memory.

I promised to do everything I could for her, said Roxanna.

The image of the dead woman did not change its expression.

You could help me a little, Roxanna continued. I only have two questions.

Suddenly the picture changed, and she saw the dead woman resting in the armchair after the policeman had picked her up from the floor. The dead woman stared at her with an expressionless face. Roxanna resisted the new image. In a way, it was artificial, created by the policeman's intervention. She would have preferred to see the dead woman as she had been found. In this respect, she herself was a victim of her insistence on sitting at eye level with the deceased.

You can return to your rest in a moment, just answer two questions for me.

Roxanna waited for a while, looking at the picture to see if anything had changed in her expression.

Do you know an Alessandro? Italian, petty book thief, specialized in the Vatican library.

The dead woman's features seemed to move for a moment. The shape of the mouth changed a little, as if the dead woman wanted to say something.

Roxanna waited until the image was completely still again before her eyes, then she asked the second question.

Michelle Denatielle, do you know this woman?

A cold shower of rain burst from the clouds, a brief gust of wind swept through the bushes, and in the swirl of dead autumn leaves the image distorted into a terrible grimace. White as a sheet, Roxanna cupped her hands to her face to erase the brief flash of expression; she had never seen a more terrifying grimace. When she removed her hands from her eyes, the grave was covered in withered leaves.

They were the same color as the carpet in the dead woman's living room. Roxanna suddenly realized it. She recognized the figure of the deceased in the restless pattern of the dead leaves. It was exactly as it had been then. Madame Richaud had been found in this position. Once again, she looked carefully at the body lying in front of her. Why hadn't she noticed it then? A line ran from the dead woman's gaze to her right arm, which lay strangely bent next to the body. Only one finger of the hand was outstretched. It seemed to be pointing to a specific spot. Roxanna closed her eyes again to memorize the image.

Thank you, Madame, rest in peace. I don't think I'll have to disturb you anymore.

Then she hurried back across the cemetery in the cold, dusky autumn shower, trying to escape from the inhospitable site before nightfall.

Madame Richaud's mansion was still sealed. At the police station, Roxanna had once again carefully studied all the photos that had been taken. Filled with these pictures, she got into her Rover and headed for the Richaud estate.

In the space of a few weeks, the well-tended garden had become a wild, overgrown landscape. The well-tended lawn had been transformed into a lush, flowering meadow, neatly trimmed hedges had mutated into disheveled mop tops and a few wild cats were perched in the old trees, staring curiously down at the visitor.

Madame Richaud had not been married, the last descendant of an established family. She had bequeathed five per cent of her vast fortune to the pizza delivery man. Now they were both dead. The state would probably extend its greedy claws and make everything disappear into the empty state coffers. It's a pity that dead people are no longer enterprising, thought Roxanna. Madame Richaud could have signed the villa over to her posthumously if she had been successful, it would have been the least she could do for her efforts. The first wild traces in the once sterile, well-tended landscape developed an attractive charm. With a disappointed sigh, she opened the sealed front door.

She might have realized it beforehand; surprised for no reason, she took a step back. In the days she had been away, someone had broken into the villa and turned everything upside down. The chalk drawing on the floor was still visible but littered with books that had been torn from the shelves.

Roxanna's spatial imagination was not the best and she decided, regardless of any traces or fingerprints, to get things in order first. Only in familiar surroundings would she have a chance of interpreting the picture with the pointing finger that had appeared in the cemetery as a meaningful trace. Half an hour later, the old order had been restored in a makeshift manner. The chalk drawing, cleared of the fallen books, lay on the carpet colored with autumn leaves, the traced arm matching the position of the picture in the cemetery with meticulous perfection.

Roxanna imagined a woman's hand on the chalk stump of the arm and let a finger stretch out in her mind.

It pointed meaninglessly to a bare spot on the wall. Discouraged, the inspector looked at the pale wallpaper, expectantly tapping the bricks underneath. She didn't really think she would find a hidden cavity and her belief didn't deceive her. She extended her outstretched finger in an imaginary straight line, let it break through the wall of the house and followed the trail into the garden. Here, too, no conspicuous features crossed her gaze. Resigned, she dropped into the armchair.

The visit to the cemetery was in vain, the study of the pictures was in vain, everything had been in vain! She chased after some connection that didn't exist anywhere except in her head. Lost in thought, she let the time pass, staring at the chalk figure on the floor from time to time.

Of course, it suddenly occurred to her. Dead people can't climb stairs. What if Madame Richaud really wanted to point to something in her death throes, but not here, not on the ground floor, perhaps in the cellar, possibly upstairs or even in the attic? Roxanna thought about it. She first decided in favor of the light-flooded first floor. Huge floor-to-ceiling windows let daylight into the rooms, which glowed in the autumn colors of whimsical nature. Roxanna looked at each room, imagining the person prostrate on the floor and tracing a line running away from the outstretched finger. In vain, not a single room revealed the secret she had hoped for.

That left the cellar and the attic. Darkness or spiders, thought Roxanna, which will you choose first? She chose the spiders. In the attic, grey webs spread out between the furniture, the vibrations of her footsteps causing dark, hairy creatures to disappear at lightning speed into hidden corners. Roxanna kept walking. She turned roughly in the direction of the dead woman's finger, tried to visualize her image and then closed her eyes.

Let yourself be guided by your feelings, she thought, for once in your life only by your feelings. It was difficult for her, she was too much influenced by her mind.

All of a sudden, the image before her eyes changed and she saw a seemingly meaningless wooden chest packed full of junk; she thought she recognized dust-covered books on the floor. With difficulty, she tried to penetrate deeper with her gaze, but the image did not change. When she opened her eyes, her gaze fell on an old cupboard as before. As she opened the door, a grey shadow flitted across her feet, fortunately it did not change direction vertically. White as a sheet, she drew in a deep breath, the dust flakes rushing into her wide-open mouth, triggering a violent coughing fit. Disgusted, she pulled tattered scraps of clothing from the wardrobe, the mouse droppings falling to the floor rustling like grains of sand. A second wooden chest appeared from under the mountain. On top were old dolls with frozen gazes, stuffed animals with eaten fur and tangled writing utensils.

She carefully slid her hand between the clutter. Any sensible mouse, any sensible spider must have left long ago, she told herself. The chest seemed strangely familiar to her, her hands dragging her through the decaying, jelly-like masses. She was not fazed. A moment later, she was holding a pigskin-covered object in her hand. When she opened it, she thought she heard the squeaking of the animal that belonged to it as she pulled off the leather casing. However, it was the creaking attic door, slowly closing, unfortunately Roxanna had not recognized the sound correctly.

Roxanna shouldn't have failed to hear the noise. In her job, you were never allowed to become so fascinated by something that you were no longer aware of anything around you.

She looked at the open book. It wasn't really a book, but rather individual pages that had been torn out of old books with surgical precision. Handwritten, with an engraved typeface. The texts were written in Latin, they remained closed to her mind, she only recognized a few words.

One of the sheets caught her attention. There were handwritten additions on it that were not part of the original text. The one handwriting had to be from the same period. It was a jittery, unsteady script, drawn with a greasy pen. Drawn by the same hand, next to the inscriptions, were hideously distorted, grimacing faces that gave the pages a sinister look. Roxanna carefully turned the page. The back was emblazoned with the vivid image of a church dignitary. The old color had lost none of its splendor, the red purple glowed like the rising sun, the precisely painted eyes poked out of the paper as if they wanted to put the viewer in wrought-iron chains forever.

Roxanna was taken aback. In the figure's mouth was the severed head of a snake. She couldn't tell for sure whether the severed torso, from which thick drops of blood were dripping onto the lips, had been added later. Possibly by the same hand that had added the grimacing heads on the front like ancient graffiti.

Next to the armchair on which the voluptuous person was enthroned, the figure of a naked woman floated on a silken feather bed. Roxanna had never seen such a beautiful figure before; the sight of her gave her the feeling of rising weightlessly from a fountain of youth. Only in her face did the beauty change into a few restless features that suggested confusion behind the facade of her expression.

Further additions had been made to the sheet in a different handwriting. Outrageously, with a simple ballpoint pen that had slipped thoughtlessly over the honorable old paper. This handwriting seemed strangely familiar to Roxanna. She had a photographic memory for details. Without question, she had seen this handwriting before. But where?

She thought hard. Of course she had. She reached into her bag and pulled out a scrap of paper. Her pockets were a graveyard for notes, Sergeant Henry had once mocked. Her former colleague, Sergeant Dudley, had been of the same opinion. It didn't bother her. Cemeteries were interesting places where you could get a lot of help. Only openness was needed, boundless openness, to benefit from this place.

She compared the writing on the note with the notes on the old pages of the book. Both were identical. She silently read the few lines on the piece of paper: Michelle Denatielle, under the name an address. She had only met this woman once before, after Alessandro's fatal accident. Out of sheer habit, she had asked this Michelle to write down her address. She refused business cards in such situations. In her own way, she got the valuable handwriting of a possible perpetrator and lots of DNA material if she asked as many people as possible to write down their own address on a piece of paper. Perhaps more questions would come up later, she had added by way of explanation. And the other questions had arisen. Now at the latest. What was Michelle Denatielle's handwriting doing on the old pages? And what were the old pages doing in the dusty attic of the late Madame Richaud?

Questions, new questions, but they got Roxanna further. There must be a connection between the dead Madame Richaud and Michelle Denatielle, and probably Alessandro, the book thief, had somehow been involved in this connection.

Suddenly, a completely different thought occurred to Roxanna. What would she herself do with such old pages? It seemed very unlikely that one of the two women, either Madame Richaud or Michelle Denatielle, had not had the old Latin texts translated, but had possibly translated them themselves. Then the translation had to be hidden somewhere in the house.

The cellar, Roxanna suddenly realized, was the only place she had not yet searched. Didn't it make sense to hide both as far away from each other as possible?

She turned around, only now realizing that the attic door had slammed shut. Probably a gust of wind. Unfortunately, she couldn't recognize the footprints that had already made their way from the attic to the cellar before her.

Madame Richaud's principle was simple once you recognized it. The translations were actually kept in the cellar, in a discarded fridge that stood in the same direction as the outstretched finger of the dead woman had pointed one floor up. In the dim light of the cellar, Roxanna skimmed over the texts translated from the old Latin.

... His soul will never find the peace he presumed to preach about. For eternity his pig-like, over fattened body will not taste the blissfully floating state of heaven, the darkness of his guilt will not leave him and the image of the beauty killed by his hatred will haunt him like a thunderous battle cry by day and by night. Who can describe the grace of your form without exposing himself in the poverty of his words, without being able to reproduce the thousandth part of what my eyes have seen? The purity of your gaze, it will never depart from the happy memories that have passed, it has become the fountain of life for my soul, from which a single drop of water has enveloped my body with refreshment and relief. What a devastating pain ravages my innermost being and will find no peace even at the hour when I will cover the laws written in me with hatred to lay hands on him. Yet I will not desire a single thought, only to rest by your side in the silence of the grave, this is my last thought dedicated to you. I will not let go of you...

The cellar door slammed shut with a heavy thud, the next moment it turned pitch black and all the lights in the house went out. Roxanna listened intently into the darkness. Behind the cellar door, she heard a soft scraping, from which a woman's malicious laughter emerged.

Well, Michelle Denatielle, how do you like that? Just a single sentence, then silence returned.

Roxanna was thinking feverishly when the voice sounded again.

You see, I love surprises too... like Australia! It cost me 10,000 euros. You'll be kind enough to reimburse me. And the 300 euros in expenses for the sleazy porter.

The woman's voice laughed again.

Admittedly, Australia was beautiful. I was stupid to fall for this simple trick. We'll have plenty of time to talk about the stupidity, Michelle Denatielle.

Michelle Denatielle, Roxanna repeated quietly.

The woman obviously thought she was Michelle Denatielle.

Listen, I'm Inspector Roxanna from the fourth police station, Roxanna replied. I don't know who you are. But it would be better if you opened the door immediately.

The voice was silent. The stranger was probably thinking. There was a long pause, then the voice was heard again.

Tell me something about yourself and what you're doing here.

The inspector thought about it. Was it a stalling tactic? Would it be better to ignore the request?

All right, replied Roxanna. I'm an inspector from the fourth police station. I'm investigating the murder of Madame Richaud. You will understand that details are subject to official secrecy. Why do you think I'm Michelle Denatielle?

Roxanna faltered.

Keep talking, the stranger shouted through the door, keep talking, keep talking, until I allow you to stop.

The stranger seemed to be a psychopath, it flashed through Roxanna's mind, and she went on to say some irrelevant stuff about colleagues like Sergeant Henry and Sergeant Dudley.

Suddenly she was interrupted by the voice.

Tell me the telephone number of your police station, the stranger demanded.

It wasn't the meaning of the words that made Roxanna freeze, but rather the sound the voice had suddenly taken on. The stranger suddenly sounded like her, the same tone of voice, the same vibrations and word melodies.

As if hypnotized, Roxanna gave her telephone number.

She heard the phone click. Shortly afterwards, she heard herself speaking outside.

Sergeant Henry, how are you? Just wanted to check in. I've got a hot lead in London. Tell the boss I have to go to London for a week immediately. That's where the key to our murder case is. If I don't find anything there, I'll spend a few days in Rome. The key is in one of these places.

There was a slight pause, then a laugh. It was unbelievable, Roxanna heard herself laughing outside the cellar door.

Of course, Sergeant Henry, you're still the same old man. Represent me well. I'll be back in a fortnight at the latest.

Then the stranger hung up the phone.

Roxanna only slowly awoke from her hypnosis. The stranger was a linguistic genius. The woman had only let her talk to memorize her voice. And then, unbelievably, the stranger had signed her, Inspector Roxanna, off duty for a week. It meant nothing other than that this psychopath was planning to lock her up in the cellar of the late Madame Richaud for a week, or forever, a week is a long way off.

But what did this sinister woman want with an uninvolved police inspector? Roxanna heard the muffled sound of footsteps moving away. She did not yet realize that it would be several days, five days, before the stranger returned. Five days and not a morsel of bread, without a drop of water, without a spark of daylight.

Exactly 20 years ago to the day, His Excellency's secretary went to the old library. For the sermon on the supreme Christian holiday, which would fall upon the faithful in three weeks' time, His Excellency was inspired – to put it in Christian terms – to fall back on something old in order to provide a bulwark against the violent innovations of the time.

A thought on celibacy or abortion, a thought on the dominance of men in the old church, a thought on apostate modern man, was it not expedient to use a thought couched in the powerful language of the forefathers to meet the upcoming high feast day in a fitting manner?

The secretary had been told to rely on intuition. So he wandered aimlessly through the magnificent rows of books, letting his eyes wander over the sturdy leather bindings and trying not to think about anything. Suddenly he stopped, closed his eyes and blackened by his own intuition, reached into the ornate shelves.

A thick book wedged itself between his fingers as he withdrew his hand. He ran to the nearest writing desk to search the chosen book for something useful at one of the old tables. His eyes ran over old Latin texts, interspersed with delicate marginal drawings depicting former church excellences. He was travelling back in time 500 years, trying to penetrate the ancient spheres more with every word. He was captivated by the splendid, overloaded baroque language and became more and more deeply entangled in the old sermons and life stories of the highly dressed church dignitaries of earlier years. Suddenly he noticed a break in the ongoing text and looked at the page number with irritation. A page was missing. His eyes fixed on the empty space; the page had been torn out with surgical precision, only the break in the text made its absence conspicuous.

His Excellency's secretary continued to turn the pages. The next page felt heavier even before he had turned it. He turned the page and looked at the picture of an old provost. He was lying prone on a silken bed, with parts of an unclothed woman's body recognizable beneath his body. The whole thing was not a hand drawing from ancient times, it was a computer-animated transcription on glossy paper, adapted to the present day. The secretary's hands trembled, and he clutched the book with difficulty. Who had committed the sacrilege of removing a page from the book? Who had committed the sacrilege of transcribing the venerable figure in this reprehensible position? He jammed his fingers into the sore spot and hurried out of the library to tell his honor the bad news.

The reaction was predictable.

Silence, commanded His Excellency, the most reverend, for heaven's sake, silence. Silence, like a grave!

The last words suddenly created a cool silence in the room; they almost had the pale flavor of a threat if the person addressed did not follow the advice.

The secretary understood. The church shunned the police like the devil shuns holy water. Police within the venerable walls. Unthinkable! Crimes may have been committed here, but there was no reason to call the police and never had been for centuries. Instead, God's justice was invoked and sent after the criminal like an invisible curse, giving the inhabitants of the old walls a clear conscience, while the invisible criminal was chased down into the dark earth by the sharp sword of justice.

One day became longer than the next. Night and day soon became indistinguishable from each other, as did thirst and hunger. Everything had melted into a black mass of fear, darkness, pain, desolation and a premonition of death.

During the first two days, Roxanna could still hear the strangers' voices, their footsteps sweeping through the house, the slamming of doors, sometimes violent noises as the contents of cupboards crashed to the floor.

Two days of dead silence followed, the sounds that had become familiar had disappeared, nothing interrupted the endless black silence of the cellar vault. Roxanna had examined every corner of the room. It was laid out like a bunker, meter-thick walls, interrupted in a few places by winding, centimeter-thin shafts to the outside, to secure the air supply in an emergency. Someone had bricked up the shafts, the only connection to the outside world. Only the cellar door connected the room to the outside; the heavy bunker door had been replaced later and let in a tolerable amount of fresh air and oxygen.

Roxanna had tracked down a single tin can in a corner of the room. In the darkness, it was impossible to make out the labelling. It took her several hours to knock a hole in the tin. A strange odor emanated from the opening, meaty, no longer fresh. It took her a long time to recognize the smell. She was reminded of the past, as a girl she owned a dog, the same aroma emanated from the dog food tins back then.

It wasn't a question of choice, even if she found it difficult. She tried to suppress her thoughts about what was in that tin, but the image of a huge tripe kept appearing in the darkness, forcing its way into the tin with smacking noises and turning there incessantly with a low rumbling noise. After the first bite, she felt like throwing up, but her emaciated body kept the unfamiliar food down. After a few minutes, she got used to the black porridge and stuffed the rest down her throat. She would have needed a whisky now to wash everything down, to disinfect her own innards with the alcohol. There was no such thing to be found and so the remains of the devoured tripe remained between her teeth for the next few hours, to be decomposed by nasty bacteria. She could still forgive the stranger for locking her up, perhaps. She would never forgive her for the dog food. There would be hundreds of ways to double the stranger's punishment. She had learnt all the tricks in the course of her professional life. But first she had to get out, leave her basement prison and put the others behind bars.

It was the fifth day when Roxanna found the can. After a few hours, she felt new strength returning to her body, but only for a short time. Afterwards, countless lead weights clung to her limbs and dragged her to the cold cellar floor. As if from far away, she heard footsteps, a key turning in a prison door. Light, the first rays of light for days, fell into the bunker room and behind it the cold face of the stranger.

Get up, the woman said, but hurry.

Get up, Roxanna repeated sarcastically, tons of lead weights hanging from her limbs. How on earth was she supposed to get up?

When she didn't move, the stranger kicked her in the side.

You don't need to pretend, she said gruffly, you police officers are well trained. Five days without food, you'll get over that in no time.

The stranger waited a moment. When the inspector still didn't move, she grabbed Roxanna's arms and dragged her up the basement stairs. Upstairs, the stranger had set up a room like a police station. She dragged Roxanna onto a chair, shone the glare of a table lamp into her eyes unaccustomed to light and lit a cigarette.

You're going to tell me all about Michelle Denatielle, the woman said.

She stared at the burning cigarette.

I might not be able to find an ashtray, she added sarcastically. That would be a shame. But let's leave it at that and get started.

Michelle Denatielle got up very early that day. Perhaps she could have bribed someone to let her past the queue and into the Vatican chambers; after all, she was in the south. She decided against it, as it could also boomerang and make those involved remember her later. When she stepped out on to the street, it was an hour before the library opened and around 200 people had already formed a queue, standing motionless in the cool morning. In front of her stood a young woman with a little boy, black hair, deep blue eyes like the sea in the south of the country. Behind a forgotten night cloud, the sun broke out wearily and warmed the bodies of the still tired people with its first rays.

In a short time, a long queue had also formed behind Michelle. After an hour, the queue slowly began to move forward. The beginning of the waiting line of people was hidden from her view behind two corners of the building, a door must have opened to swallow the waiting people into the old walls in its gaping jaws.

Michelle didn't need to move her legs, she let herself be pulled along by the gentle suction of the queue rolling forwards and after 20 minutes stood in front of the sterile, sober entrance door of the museum complex. She disoriented herself to familiarize herself with the premises. After closing, large cleaning crews would no doubt be rolling through the state rooms, especially the entrance area and the sanitary facilities. It was too cheap to hide here, who knows how many had tried before her.

Michelle let herself drift further away from the crowd. The bodies of people poured through the old rooms like a sluggish stream. The walls were overloaded with huge paintings, in some rooms not a single spot remained uncovered by the gold-framed pictures, one more magnificent than the next. Just when the overwhelmed senses thought they could see no further increase, even more ornate works appeared in the next room and crashed down on the viewer with the weight of their perfection. Michelle forgot her actual intention. With each painting, she immersed herself in the past, the people depicted began to vibrate in the heat of the summer day, in the glowing air, and set themselves in motion. They spoke to each other in strange sounds, accompanied by sparse, well-formed gestures. The depicted objects fell from the screen and built themselves up in the narrow corridors, more real than reality.

An indescribable feeling, a mixture of happiness, fascination, curiosity and much more, spread through Michelle. She floated through the rooms as if in a trance, everything around her was deserted, only the old figures that had come to life surrounded her. Michelle was only startled when she was swept away into a huge, wood-paneled room. Shelves had been erected in front of the walls with the meticulousness of guardsmen, overflowing with old, leather-bound books.

Michelle suddenly woke up, the reason for her visit flashed through her mind, pulling her out of the unreal world and into the sober surroundings of the other visitors standing around her, sweating in the sun's heat.

Thousands of books waited behind glass shelves, Michelle was drawn to the hidden ancient knowledge like an invisible magnet. How was she supposed to find the right one in the infinity of written pages? She consoled herself that every failed attempt would immerse her more in the ancient world. She had also prepared herself and was able to narrow down quite well where she needed to look in the hall.

Now she just had to find a hiding place for herself so that she could find the other secret, her counterpart, in the night when the old rooms had been swept clean and the people who had come to life had sunk back into sleep. She had a good feeling, since this morning she knew it was going to be a good day. And at last she had identified a place in the huge complex of buildings that would swallow her up until the darkness of night. Soon, not much longer, and she would have the secret in her hands.

We have the same interests, said the stranger, looking down indifferently at the inspector. You are a woman of honor.

She laughed briefly.

A woman of honor, well, that kind of feeling wasn't to be found today. Better to say: you're a woman of honor who keeps her word. At least I think so. Your eyes give it away. They are curious, but not devious. You lack the usual companion of ambition. You are just single-minded but won't walk over dead bodies.

The stranger laughed again.

Sometimes in your profession perhaps you do, in the literal sense. You walk over dead bodies. That's okay. You honestly walk over dead bodies, that speaks in your favor.

The stranger paused for a moment, then continued.

I don't want to hold a monologue. Your freedom for my freedom... and some information.

Roxanna thought about it. Her word would bind her, the stranger was right, and she trusted the other to run away, to let a police inspector starve miserably.

I will forget everything. Everything that has happened in the last few days. You have my word.

The stranger nodded with relief.

You're sensible. In your position, I would be sensible too. But you are, because you're clever. What do you think about my other condition?

The information? Roxanna asked back.

Yes, some information. You see, we're both after the same person. I propose a fair deal. You give me your information, and I'll share some of my knowledge, then I'll let you go.

What are you going to do with Michelle Denatielle when you find her? You're looking for this Michelle Denatielle.

I didn't underestimate you, the stranger replied. At first, I thought it was Michelle Denatielle who had come into the house. It was quite a surprise when I realized that I had been caught by a policewoman instead. What would you have done in my place?

I probably would have just left, Roxanna replied. I would have left the door locked and left. A halfway normal policewoman can get out of a locked door. It would have been the best solution for both of us.

Past, interrupted the other. Let's leave what happened. What do you think about the second part, the exchange of information?

Roxanna realized that without this part of the condition, there would be no freedom for her. Reluctantly, she agreed.

I don't seem to have an alternative.

The stranger confirmed her assumption and even went a little further. Suddenly she stood up and untied Roxanna's wrists and ankles.

Sit down, the stranger suddenly said in an exaggeratedly friendly manner. Let's talk a little about this Michelle Denatielle. I think we'll all benefit from it.

Before Roxanna knew it, she was involved in a casual conversation. Later, she marveled at how candidly she had revealed some of the details of her investigation so far. The stranger must have been psychologically trained. Imperceptibly, she had transformed the threatening atmosphere of the past few days into the coziness of a chat over coffee between two middle-aged women. Perhaps it was the renunciations of the past few days that made Roxanna react in this way. She was a communicative person; she hadn't spoken to anyone for several days. The conversation was like a return to life.

After a few minutes, the stranger interrupted the conversation. She had obviously obtained all the essential information. Abruptly, Roxanna returned to reality as if from a hypnotized state.

You didn't answer my question from earlier, Roxanna interjected into the silence. What do you want to do with Michelle Denatielle?

There was a long pause. Finally, when Roxanna no longer expected an answer, she replied.

I was in Australia. Had some expenses. I owe the trip to that Michelle Denatielle. I just want to recover my expenses. With expenses.

Roxanna understood. From now on, the game was back to face-down cards.

Allow me one last question, the inspector asked. This Alessandro, did you know him?

The stranger didn't respond. Suddenly a few tears rolled out of her right eye. She stood up without a word. She held out her hand to the inspector.

I apologize for the circumstances. Nevertheless, it was a pleasure to meet you. When it comes to a dangerous woman, we women should stick together.

You see, that's the difference. It never works with men. Hitler, Stalin, Mao, all those insane, barmy tyrants, they would have been nothing but a pile of shit if the other men had stuck together. We women should do it differently.

Without another word, the stranger turned round, crossed the room with springy steps and floated away like an angel. Roxanna was left alone. Were there only crazy people left on this rotating globe?

From her safe hiding place, Michelle Denatielle heard the sounds of the cleaning crew hurriedly sweeping through the rooms. Only rare snatches of Italian words reached her ears; the hidden confusion lasted a few minutes until the sounds of work and scraps of speech had disappeared. She had prepared herself well and knew about the night watchman's tour in an hour's time. She was fit and would be able to cope with this time in her cramped hiding place.

In front of her eyes, a few people still floated alive from the magnificent paintings, their glittering capes twinkling like stars in the Italian night sky. Lost in thought, she daydreamed until she suddenly heard footsteps coming directly towards her.

Michelle Denatielle held her breath; it could only be the night watchman on his routine rounds. The footsteps accelerated, paused just before the hiding place, there were a few minutes of absolute silence and then the night figure moved away again.

To be on the safe side, Michelle Denatielle waited another five minutes before crawling out of her hiding place. She had barely entered the dark library when she noticed something strange through the windows. As if at the push of a button, the lights of the city at her feet went out and from one moment to the next, Rome had disappeared into a black pool. Her instincts had not deceived her. It was going to be a good day for her. And she needed her gut feeling now. Wasn't everything in this huge building

complex based on feeling, on intuition? Why should-
n't she use these tools where they were at home?

She paced devoutly through the rows of darkened
books. Detached, she waited for a certain feeling
that would make her legs stop. She didn't have to
wait long. A gentle warmth flooded her chest, turning into an unprecedented heat that made her face
glow in the black night. With a steady hand, she
reached for the book that was directly in front of her
at eye level; like a marker, it had advanced a few cen-
timeters from the row of other volumes, as if it were
already awaiting the visitor. An ornate bookmark
made from cut-off women's hair divided the book.
When Michelle opened it at the marker, she knew
immediately by the light of the torch that she had
found what she was looking for straight away.

Using a scalpel, she removed three pages, closed the
heavy book and put it back on the shelf. She had
barely put the volume back when she suddenly
heard the same footsteps as before. She switched
off the torch and hurried back into the hiding place.
Her heavy breathing moistened the black air, and
the footsteps came straight towards her again.

This time they did not pause. They approached inex-
orably, still not stopping until they bumped hard
against the hiding place. A stranger's hand reached
for the door and yanked it open. A bright beam of
light flashed into Michelle Denatielle's eyes. A man
was standing in front of her; despite the dim lighting,
she could recognize him clearly. It hit her like a bolt
of lightning. The man resembled this Alessandro
down to the tips of his hair, but this Alessandro, he

had fallen to his death through the open lift floor weeks ago. Now he was standing opposite her in the Vatican library, in the middle of the night, and outside the city lay in the dark pool of the blackout.

You look worn out, Roxanna. No luck?

Sergeant Dudley grinned. He had seven days' rest behind him. Roxanna didn't need to think that he had put in much effort in her absence. His best helper was time. Some crimes solved themselves by chance, others sank into the disinterest of the past. All he had to do was sit in h s office, sit and wait until time had decided in favor of one of the two paths. Why undertake these arduous journeys like the inspector?

Roxanna nodded.

It was a bit much, you're right.

Who tied you up? Dudley asked.

Roxanna cringed inwardly. Only now did she notice the welts on her wrists; Dudley had noticed them immediately.

Nobody, Roxanna replied dryly, what makes you think that?

Dudley was silent. But only for a moment.

I've been a policeman longer than you have. I'm not your superior officer, all right, but tell me who tied you up. Or did you discover the maso trip?

Can you keep quiet, Dudley?

The sergeant replied in the affirmative.

You mustn't betray me. You know our boss. I spent two days of the trip with my brother in London. Privately, you understand. A business trip and two days on a private side trip. Doesn't read well in a report, does it? Believe it or not. I had to play cops and robbers with my nephew for a whole day. You wouldn't believe how brutal boys are when they get their hands on a real policewoman. Well, it was fun too. Just switch off, forget everything, this lousy office, our boss, the three dead people, nobody can see through it anyway.

Shall we close the file? Dudley asked. I hear you haven't been able to find out anything new anyway. Then your first theory applies. You've already written the protocol. You just need to fill in the blanks. I didn't understand why you left these big gaps in the protocol anyway. Just close the case, the next murder is sure to come. New game, new luck.

You're right, Dudley. Sometimes you're just right. It's good to know you can keep quiet.

About the two days?
Roxanna nodded.

I can keep quiet, that's true, Dudley repeated. You're in the police force. You should have learnt by now that all these crimes are about performance and reward. I mean, two days of playing with children at the state's expense.
Dudley laughed out loud.

Of course I'll keep quiet. And in twenty years I'll be silent as the grave. But you, you'll spend a week, you see, that's seven long days, you'll spend a week making the coffee for the whole police station.
Dudley grinned. He knew how much Roxanna hated this. He also knew that he had won a small victory. And he savored the feeling.

You know, Dudley, Roxanna replied. Do you know how many people are murdered undetected? The best method is still arsenic with coffee. I think a week will be enough.

But then I want to die in your arms, Dudley burst out. At the station, here on duty. And you, Roxanna, you close my eyes.

Dudley became melancholy.

My mum used to do that to me as a child, every night. And don't forget to write the obituary for old Dudley. You have imagination and literary talent. Your protocols read like a novel.

Dudley looked at Roxanna, then continued smugly.

Like a novel, even the contents.

A few minutes passed before Michelle Denatielle came round. Stunned, she stared at the man standing in front of her in the dark. Only the cone of light from the torch illuminated the outline of the figure.

You'll think I'm crazy, Michelle stuttered, but can I touch you once? Otherwise, I can't believe you're not a ghost.

The man allowed her to do so.

Don't force yourself.

But no nasty tricks.

Only now did Michelle see that the man was holding an opened knife in his right hand. It was pointed directly at her. Nevertheless, she stretched her arm forwards and tapped the man on the shoulder. She could actually feel something. In front of her stood this Alessandro, who had fallen to his death from her flat lift.

In my job, you better have two lives, the man said. There comes a time when you need a second life.

You weren't dead? It's impossible to survive the fall.

You don't say. I assume you've thought everything through very carefully. How many did you get rid of that way?

Nobody, Michelle replied, not even you. It was an accident. Believe me.

I believe it was, but the police didn't. This inspector is still investigating, it could become unpleasant for you.

The man held up the knife.

Look, if they find you dead here. No one will think of a certain Alessandro. Dead men don't kill. It's simple, isn't it? Don't worry about the accident, it didn't cost me a single broken bone.

I don't understand.

We did everything together, the man replied. At some point we had to choose a career. Alessandro the First opted for criminal. So, the decision for me, for Alessandro the Second, was clear. A deal, you understand? I was allowed to choose our first girlfriend together and my brother was allowed to choose our first profession together.

Your brother?

More precisely, twin brother. My second life. You see, everyone needs a second life at some point. It's a shame about Alessandro. But I've got into the habit of looking at everything soberly. Since his death, I'm twice as rich as I used to be. I no longer have half a wife and, Alessandro sighed, I now have to work twice as much. And I owe it all to you.

The whole woman must be that Alessia, Michelle burst out.

Look, you're damn clever. Too clever, hissed the stranger.

At the same moment, he raised the flashing knife into the black night.

Roxanna learnt about the crime from the newspaper. In Italy, all the papers were plastered with it, like a dangerous, disgusting rash. Abroad, the publicity was less violent, but enough to catch the eye of a reasonably attentive reader.

Death in the Vatican.

Blood on history (probably meaning the venerable old books, now stained with blood).

Many other headlines writhed like black snakes across the newsprint, with the text about the incident printed in blood red underneath.

Roxanna only realized why she had been magically drawn to the event after she had intuitively bought a few Italian newspapers at the station to find out more about the crime. The victim was pictured on some of the pages. She recognized it immediately, the facts of the murder case with the three dead people automatically running through her head. It couldn't be possible. But Roxanna had learnt that the impossible in her job turned out to be the most natural thing in the world.

Her boss would not authorize another business trip to Rome. That much was clear. She picked up the phone and tried to contact the Italian police station responsible. It was like an odyssey. It wasn't until late afternoon that she reached the right place. But then Roxanna was immediately intrigued. Half a day had been enough for the Italian police to solve the case.

The victim was a self-sacrifice, a certain Alessandro. Four days ago, he had hired himself out as a night watchman in the Vatican Museums. Presumably to obtain certain pages from valuable old books for unknown clients by simply cutting them out with a sharp knife.

This Alessandro worked together with his twin brother, who fell to his death a few weeks ago through an open lift floor. Presumably the last Alessandro had realized that he was being tracked down. A letter had recently arrived at police headquarters from a Vatican office informing them of a book crime. As it was important not to cause a stir, a special surveillance of the Vatican library was being organized for the next week. This criminal would have been caught by then at the latest. Now he had executed himself, hara-kiri style, by ramming a knife into his stomach.

That's how it must have been, colleagues, said the voice at the other end. We have absolutely no indication that there was another person at the scene of the crime.

But why would someone be employed as a night watchman in a world-famous library, secretly steal pages of books and theatrically kill himself one night?

Perhaps his conscience, answered the Italian police voice. You see, this Alessandro was a Catholic. He separates some pages from an old church book. That's good. Not for the first time. Good. Suddenly his conscience tells him that he is stealing from the Catholic Church. Not good. Thoughts of purgatory and hell arise in his head. Not good either. Remorse. Good. Too late? What do I know, call it repentance. With the knife with which he killed the books, he cut out their hearts, with this knife he kills himself. Good or not good. But that's how it must have happened. Roxanna understood, that is, she didn't really understand, well, she did understand. The whole affair had to be boiled down as quickly as possible. In Italy, especially in the Vatican, there was a great deal of interest in not blowing the matter out of proportion. A theatrical suicide out of remorse, at night at the scene of the outrage, had something penitential, something pathetic about it.

Vigilante justice in the most authentic sense. Moreover, there was actually no evidence of a murder. And the Vatican was not interested in any criminal theories. Every book in the huge library had to be leafed through carefully, page by page, to find out where something was missing. There was also the not insignificant question of whether there was a connection between the missing pages and, nobody dared to think it , whether some not entirely pleasant parts of past church history had been touched on here.

Logistical preparations also had to be made. The press presentation would multiply the already immense number of daily visitors to the museum, many of whom would come to see the scene of the strange events in the library and let a pleasant cool shiver run down their spines in the heat of the late Italian summer.

Hello, are you still there? The voice asked in rapid Italian.

Only now did Roxanna realize that she was still on the phone to Rome. Her thoughts had taken her far away. She was still on the phone, certainly, but not as close to the case as before. Everything had become more confused.

Yes, thank you for your help, she said briefly. Thank you very much. If you ever need help in London, just give us a call. We'll return the favor.

Hardly, the voice ended in a put-upon tone, or do you have such an interesting library in London?

That was the end of the conversation.

In the evening Roxanna went to Harry's bar. It was the best place to switch off and she also had a brilliant idea. The dark room was barely half full. Strange, empty tables everywhere, she had never seen Harry's bar like this before.

As usual, Inspector?
In front of Roxanna stood the boss himself, who didn't miss the opportunity to greet the inspector. There was a strange symbiosis between the underworld and the upper world in this place, and Harry, the boss, was the mediator who was fully recognized by both sides.

You travelled a long way, Rome, Italy, I heard. And on the way back, a detour to the family in London, Harry teased.
Roxanna looked up. So, Sergeant Dudley, that bastard, hadn't been able to keep his mouth shut. She should have realized that beforehand. Tomorrow he could make his own coffee again, couldn't he, or arsenic after all?

As always, Inspector, the landlord repeated.
She made a tired attempt to save herself.

I don't know where I am or where I work anymore anyway. International cases, international murders, investigations in Paris, investigations in London, contact with Rome, the whole world needs me. As if I could save the world.
Harry wasn't listening carefully.

As usual, Inspector? The landlord repeated like a stereotype once again.

Roxanna shook her head.

Ten times the usual, she replied. As always, yes, but ten times.

Harry didn't understand.

Bring me a bottle of whisky, full to the top, Roxanna ordered, or I'll have this bloody dive shut down. And when the bottle is empty, call a taxi! Do you understand?

Are you expecting company? the landlord asked, I mean, a whole bottle! You women can hardly take anything anyway. It's scientifically proven, by the way. It was in the newspaper yesterday.

I am my visitor, interrupted Roxanna. Need to discuss something with myself. If that crazy Sergeant Dudley calls for me, tell him to take his service revolver and shoot himself with it. Do you understand? That's an order. For you and for Dudley.

Harry was taken aback.

Trouble?

Roxanna didn't respond directly.

If Dudley calls, give him another order. Tell him and Sergeant Henry to line up opposite each other, each with his pistol, and pull the trigger at the same time. That's even better.

Harry shook his head. Obviously, Roxanna had already had a drink. He didn't want to imagine the orders after an empty bottle of whisky.

He had a whisky bottle for such cases, which had a glass pane on the inside, quite high up, double bottom, with only water underneath. Most drunks in their state didn't realize that the whisky bottle was empty, even though it was still three-quarters full.

He would put one of these Potemkin bottles in front of Roxannna.

None of your half-fakes, you understand, Harry, you can leave your water mirage in the cupboard.

Harry nodded silently. For a drunk, Roxanna could still think surprisingly well – or she had drunk herself into a detached state of nirvana in which she could read other people's thoughts with ease.

I would never dare with you, Harry replied. You're a woman. And a policewoman to boot. Not a pleasant combination for someone like me.

Stop this nonsense and get out of here, Roxanna said rather loudly, I have to talk to myself.

The whisky bottle was already half empty when the mobile rang. Roxanna cursed. She had forgotten to switch off this wretched thing, this incarnation of a human pain in the arse.

Inspector Roxanna, hello?

Roxanna struggled to get a few words out, the caller responded quickly.

I'm honoring our agreement, said a female voice. The exchange of information, if you understand.

Roxanna understood immediately. It was the stranger; she had been in this woman's power for over a week.

All right, replied Roxanna. You needn't think that I was idle. For a short time, you were more than half a woman.

What do you mean?

You were Alessandro's wife. And you were also Alessandro's wife. Twice half a woman. For a few weeks you were only the wife of the last Alessandro.

The strange voice swallowed.

Believe it or not, I didn't realize it for the first few years. I realized it by a stupid coincidence. Then I decided to keep playing the game. When the first Alessandro died, it didn't bother me. If you looked closely, he was completely different from his twin brother in the important aspects of love. But I brought him home. The last honor. His brother couldn't even be at the funeral. From that point on, he acted as if he no longer existed either. That hit me hard, you know?

Yes, Roxanna replied, I can understand you. And then you saw his picture in an Italian newspaper.

Dead, dead in the Vatican library. Must have been terrible.

The strange voice gulped again. Roxanna took advantage of the pause.

Listen Alessia, don't let hate drive you. Maybe this Michelle Denatielle killed the first Alessandro. Who knows? It could have been an accident, the lift hatch could have been open by mistake. We'll never know. But you have no proof that Michelle Denatielle killed her second Alessandro.

You really haven't been idle, the other woman replied. How long have you known that I and the other woman are the same person?

Some time ago, replied Roxanna. I just don't understand what you and Michelle Denatielle are after. I'll find out, Alessia, I'm sure I will, I'm sure I will.

There was a long pause. Roxanna could no longer speak. During the first few minutes she had been surprisingly well composed for half a bottle of whisky. Now everything was just spinning, and this conversation seemed unreal and alien to her.

She beckoned Harry over and pressed the mobile phone into his hand. Then she slumped over, feeling nauseous and vomiting in a wave-like gush. Harry cursed. As the vomit dripped onto his shoes, he heard the voice on the other end of the phone.

Are you all right?

Yes, yes, Harry replied. I mean, I am. Excuse me, please. The inspector just pressed her mobile phone into my hand. I think she's in a pretty bad way.

Tell her to get well soon, the woman said.

From whom, I mean, she'll ask me, from whom? Who knows if she remembers the beginning of your conversation.

Say from Alessia. Get well soon from Alessia. Who am I actually talking to?

Harry, the man replied. I'm the boss of Harry's pub. Roxanna is one of my best regulars.

Fine, replied the woman, then please remember something else. When the inspector is back together, give her this message. She'll be interested.

Just a moment, Harry interjected, I'll make a note to be on the safe side.

He picked up a piece of paper and pen and reached for the phone again.

Here we go, he said hastily.

Write the following: forget the week at Madame Richaud's house, no repetition, I recommend you go back there in three days, on the 13th. It will be a short visit this time.

Harry was busy writing.

Which house do you mean, shouldn't I make a note of the address? Listen, isn't it better to write down the address, I'm just saying.

It was no use. The other end of the line was now as dead as a three-day-old corpse. The woman had simply hung up.

From then on events came thick and fast.

A few days later, it was a Thursday, and Roxanna was sitting in her stuffy office. Sergeant Dudley came in.

Phone call for you, unfortunately in my office.

Then put it through, Roxanna replied gruffly.

You know I can't cope with the system. It's better if you go over there before I put the call through.

You stay here, Roxanna ordered and hurried across the corridor.

Hello, Inspector, this is Harry.

Roxanna was surprised.

What's going on? Have I forgotten to have a drink at your place for a week?

No, stuttered Harry. It's just because of last time.

What about last time, it was the same as always. Only your place was a bit empty.

Harry realized that the inspector had forgotten everything. He could end the conversation now with some triviality. But it didn't seem advisable to him.

A woman called for you. Alessia or something.

Roxanna became wide awake.

What did she want?

All right, said Harry. I'll tell you everything. But you have to promise not to rip my head off and to remain my regular guest.

Don't act so scared, Harry, what's happened?

I was supposed to pass something on to you. I completely forgot. Well, I had to clean up the vomit and have you driven home.

What do you mean by that, Harry?

Never mind, the man replied. Anyway, I should tell you that you should go to a woman's house on the 13th. You would already know, and you needn't be afraid, said this Alessia. It would be a short visit this time.

Roxanna fell silent. Today was already the 15th.

I'll stay a regular, Roxanna cursed into the phone, unfortunately you have the best whisky. But next time I'll rip your damn head off myself. What do you need your thick skull for when it's all going through the sieve?

Harry's tone became even softer, although the inspector would calm down again. He knew her too well.

Tell me the next time you come, he whispered. I'll take the day off. I've got so many muscles that there's no room under my arm to carry a torn-off head.

All right, Harry, a month of free drinks is the least you can do.

Let's say anything over two whiskies, Harry negotiated. Believe me, I have to live too.

Agreed, replied Roxanna, I wanted to cut down on the drinking anyway. Otherwise, my head will soon be a sieve like your lump of memory.

That was the end of the conversation.

Roxanna went back to her office, gathered together the most important things, threw indefinable things at Sergeant Dudley, who only replied something about a private business trip, and Roxanna set off on the long drive to Madame Richaud's house.

You're lucky, said the pale doctor. It was my hobby.

Roxanna agreed with him. The coroner was on the scene in no time. You could feel that death was clinging to every fibre of this man's being. Nothing could frighten him anymore.

I'll show you something, he said, provided you want it and have strong nerves. But don't throw up all over my suit. It wouldn't be the first time.

Roxanna nodded. The doctor fetched a torch and put it in the inspector's hand.

Shine it right on the mouth, he ordered, especially when I hold the jaws apart.

His gloved arms pushed apart the rigid jawbones of the dead woman, two fingers disappeared into the black jaws. When they reappeared, they were holding a strange object.

Decomposing for several days, said the doctor, pointing to the roundish object. A snake's head, with a little imagination you can recognize anything.

Roxanna felt sick. But the doctor looked at her sharply.

No vomit, he said, I can stand anything but vomit. Or at least tell me what you've eaten in the last few hours so that I can prepare myself.

That's all right, Roxanna replied tersely. Certainly, you want to explain something to me.

The doctor bent down and picked up a sinuous structure from the floor.

The rest, he explained. You see, these snakes are my hobby. Hardly anyone knows them. They're real night hunters, trained on human saliva. Ancient art, familiar only to a few initiates. You set the thing out in the room and all you have to do is wait. The black snake looks for its victim at night while it sleeps, but it is considerate. The victim feels nothing. The animal crawls up the sleeping body and waits until the sleeping person opens his mouth. It doesn't happen often during sleep, but it does happen. Everyone opens their mouth some time in their sleep. Old human disease.

If only there were people who could keep their mouths shut at night, the doctor thought. He must have been thinking of a certain person.

In any case, at the same moment, it thrusts forward into the throat like lightning and bites into the back of the palate. The victim is killed instantly. And the jaws fall down like a guillotine. This was a popular method in the Middle Ages. Nobody looks in the mouth of a deceased for a snake's head. The severed body of the reptile was easy to remove the next morning, covering all traces.

Roxanna understood. This Michelle Denatielle lay before her in the house of the dead Madame Richaud. She had died in a little-known medieval procedure. Michelle Denatielle had been interested in the Middle Ages and especially in some records from the Vatican library. This stranger, Alessia, had kept her word about sharing information and had sent the detective to the scene of the crime.

Thank you very much, Doc, said Roxanna. I have another place to visit. It's not in your district. But I'd appreciate it if you'd accompany me.

The doctor nodded. I'll apply for a business trip and let you know tomorrow. Is there time until tomorrow?

Roxanna replied in the affirmative.

I think so!

If her theory was correct, it was too late anyway, or rather, still in time. She would go to Michelle De-natielle's flat tomorrow. Not via the lift, that was too dangerous. She had the unmistakable feeling that it would be better to have this strange doctor with his specialized knowledge with her.

Roxanna had already been back at the office for a week when her boss returned from holiday. On the first day, he was unresponsive and first had to get an idea of everything that had happened in his absence. That much was clear. But the next day, the storm would break over her. She didn't even have a new murder case to investigate to get away from her boss for a few days. Not even the criminals could be relied on. If you needed them, they let you down.

Well, mate, tomorrow you're going to the scaffold.

Sergeant Dudley grinned maliciously, and Sergeant Henry willingly joined him. Henry ran into the small kitchen and came back with a fresh-smelling pizza. Dudley fetched a coffee that had just been brewed.

Tuna pizza with black coffee, your last meal, they both sneered in synchronized tones. They had obviously staged everything precisely.

Roxanna tucked into the meal. She had just finished eating when the door flew open. Her boss rushed in, furious, his face glowing. And he wanted to see her immediately, on his first day back. None of this boded well.

Roxanna slunk out of the office like a sacrificial lamb, her boss following her like a bull gone wild, while Dudley and Henry followed the procession with astonished eyes.

Chief Inspector Clanough was an old bear, normally exuding his calm over the entire office and threatening to let everything sink into lethargy. Today he was more like a bear that had forgotten its skin and tried to plunder a honey nest in such a pathetic state.

You must have gone crazy, hissed Clanough. What do you mean crazy? Mad as a hatter! Out of your mind!

Roxanna remained silent.

You travel to a foreign country without authorization! You don't inform the local police! You take a coroner outside his district!

He wanted to apply for a business trip beforehand, Roxanna interjected apologetically.

Apply beforehand? You do know people! That doctor is the craziest bloke there is! Even I've heard of him! Are you telling me you seriously believed his words?

Roxanna was silent again.

England, Italy, France, do you realize that there are still borders in Europe? Invisible ones! But much more dangerous than the visible ones! You simply ignore everything!

Roxanna remained silent.

Even though everything revolves around the Vatican! Do you have any idea what this could lead to? The only thing missing was that you would have implicated bureaucratic Germany! Unthinkable!

Roxanna thought it best to let the torrent of words wash over her and wait and see.

Suddenly the mood changed. Chief Inspector Clanough was a criminalist through and through. Now his interest in how Roxanna had solved the case came to the fore. The inspector immediately sensed the turnaround.

How did you know that you would find this Alessia in Michelle Denatielle's flat?

Instinct, replied Roxanna, and experience, ten years of experience under your leadership.
That was thick honey and the old bear Clanough smiled.

And that crazy Doc, you could only have taken him with you if you knew that Alessia had died the same way.

Correctly combined, Roxanna agreed.

Nevertheless, many questions remain unanswered, Clanough continued. Who killed the two of them? We absolutely must find a murderer.

They got rid of each other, Roxanna replied. I assume that they discovered the old secret of this strange liquidation at the same time. Each knew the other's whereabouts and where they had hidden this deadly weapon.

Well, if that's what happened, I still don't understand the motives of the two women.
Neither do I. Roxanna thought. Both were interested in the Middle Ages. Both were interested in the Vatican library. Both must have discovered the same secret at the same time.

The black snake thing was just a side issue. I think so. It was part of it, but it wasn't the main focus.

Did you find the old pages from the Vatican books? Clanough asked. Maybe that's where the secret lies.

Part of them, Roxanna replied. They are already back in Rome to appease the Italians and the Curia.

If I know you, you've made copies.

Roxanna nodded and reached into her bag.

I found the story of a provost and his concubine, a gypsy, sorry, a simple maid. An old love triangle, because the provost's servant also had a crush on the maid. At the end of his life, the provost got rid of the concubine, he begrudged her to his servant.

With a snake? interrupted Clanough spellbound.

No, he simply laid his massive body on top of the woman and suffocated her, so to speak. But the provost, he was killed by a black snake.

Both women came from good backgrounds. Let's assume the following: Neither had to work. They had inherited enough. Both were doing genealogical research out of boredom and came across the same story.

That would make sense, Clanough decided, but there's no link.

Wait a minute, Roxanna interrupted. They find out by chance, or someone tells them, that they're descended from these lines. For example, this Michelle Denatielle finds out that she comes from the Provost's line and this Alessia finds out that her line comes from the Servant.

Chief Inspector Clanough shook his head.

I don't understand anything anymore.

Just a hunch, Chief, continued Roxanna. So, someone's telling the two women the connection between their lineages, Roxanna repeated.

Interesting theory, Clanough marveled. And as a descendant of the servant, Alessia was interested in taking belated revenge on Michelle Denatielle. Michelle was a descendant of this provost, and he was responsible for the fact that her ancestor had become a murderer because the provost had killed the servant's secret lover.

Convoluted, simply convoluted, Clanough shook his head. And do you seriously think that two women would suddenly take revenge on each other because of such old stories? It's long past the statute of limitations. Then everyone could very soon have a reason to kill someone. Who knows how we're all connected.

Women are unpredictable, Roxanna replied. People have been hunted down for more trivial things. Maybe everything was completely different. The women discovered the secret of the black snakes, got hold of the creatures and happened to fall victim to their dangerous toy at the same time. The pizza delivery man wanted to kill Madame Richaud out of greed and, in his agitation, accidentally bit into the wrong half of the pizza.

And at the sight of his death, Madame Richaud died of grief and anguish over her lost lover. Like in a good fairy tale? Clanough asked sarcastically.

Yes, Roxanna confirmed, exactly that.

But then the first Alessandro was really just the victim of a tragic accident when he fell through the open hatch in the lift. And his twin brother bumped into Michelle Denatielle in the library at night purely by chance. He was actually expecting to bump into Alessia again, as she had taken over his brother's job. Instead, he finds himself face to face with Michelle Denatielle, is completely confused, feels exposed and heroically plunges a knife into his own chest.

Clanough slammed the file cover shut with a resounding bang.

Let the dead rest, he said. Either everyone has killed themselves, then we don't need to look for a murderer anymore. Or one has done away with the other. Everyone is dead, everyone would have received their punishment.

Agreed, Roxanna replied. Now please excuse me. She was in a hurry because she wanted to continue studying the copies of the old book pages. Even if it was irrelevant, perhaps she could still find an explanation of how everything was really connected.

You are leaving me alone with this disaster, Clanough called after her. The press, politicians, the police inspector, I'm supposed to take it all on my old shoulders?

You're a few pay grades above me for that. Roxanna turned round.

When it's all over, I'll invite you round. To Harry's bar. They have the best whisky there.

Clanough felt flattered. He already saw himself at a bar with a good-looking, vital woman in her forties, enjoying the jealous glances of the other men. On top of that, Roxanna would pay for the expensive whisky.

Roxanna smiled. She could read her boss's eyes. And he certainly didn't know that she had the first two whiskies free. Drinking more wasn't healthy anyway. She would convince Clanough of that. The secret of the precious lies hidden in its rarity. Two was a rare number compared to the astronomical figures that had been circulating around the world for the last few years.

The End

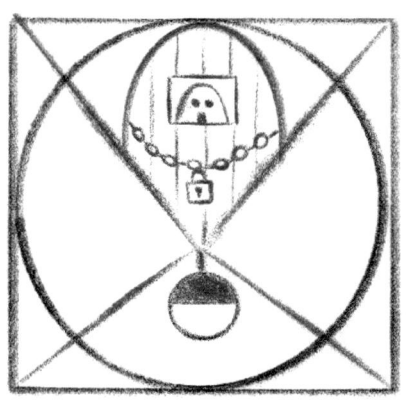

Biographical afterword

Renier-Fréduman Mundil (pseudonym) was a doctor for over forty years. During this time, he had to fight many battles, even without being a soldier. Battles with Death. With victory or defeat as the outcome or a draw in the form of a postponement until a replay, so to speak.

If Death has lost the battle, you can be one hundred per cent sure that he will request a replay at an unknown location. Not a very fair loser. Humans are also prone to such replays. The First World War was lost by one side, and at some point enough people were so dissatisfied with the result that a second "'match"' was started without further ado, even if the opponent did not want to compete and insisted on the original result. Unfortunately, the impression nowadays is that more and more people are dissatisfied with the (late) result of the second 'replay' and that all bad things come in threes.

But let's not indulge in such thoughts any longer. R.-F. Mundil has also been married for over forty years and has 25 children (four of his own, four children-in-law and seventeen grandchildren), which means that the number of children has finally reached the number of birthdays in the autumn month in which he was born.

50% of a body can be explained by chemical processes and 50% by physical processes, if you divide the processes up to the nanomechanical level, to which forensic scientists can no longer object at some point. That's why a capable police inspector should also be a good chemist and a good physicist. The rest of the whole, the soul, which, to stick with forensic jargon, is freed by death from the prison of an imperfect body, is not understood by anyone anyway, not by science, not by spiritual science and not even by religion. This remnant of the soul can only be understood through life. Presumably, even if it sounds gruesome in the final analysis, this is best understood through the end, the last step of life. Murder, as is often the basis of crime novels, is reprehensible, among other things, because it often ends life in a fraction of a second and takes away the chance to understand the most precious thing, the soul, in the last step (dying). But don't worry, the soul cannot be destroyed, no matter what weapon death deploys, it is immortal and will not be lost to us. That is why we cannot lose ourselves after the last step of life. Let's leave it at that, it's starting to get too complicated, like an entangled murder mystery.

Biography

After graduating from high school in Berlin, I studied medicine in Berlin and Munich and worked in medicine for around 40 years after my studies. I have been retired since the end of 2022. During my professional career I also wrote some manuscripts, a book for young people, children's books, novels and poems. Some have since been self-published.

In addition the author has published several novels in English translation:

Manu's Journey With Death
- A fugue through time

A life, narrated on several levels, accompanied in its tracks and followed by death. In some places, points of this life that have long since passed light up, a brief glowing breath where it pauses for a moment before it is dragged on by the stream of life and disappears somewhere, not without trace but forever. What remains? In any case, death, even if no one is interested in the remnants of this trace of life.

The Island of Figures
Youth Novel

A little girl in Japan receives a doll from her father for her birthday. When the girl is older, the doll is placed on the waves of the sea in a small boat. Apparently a tradition to mark the transition to a new phase of life into adulthood.

Some time later, another girl travels after her missing doll, and an exciting, adventurous journey begins with an unusual, surprising end

Chrystillian Christmas –
Christmas as usual ~~and~~ different

A goose on its flight to baking-oven land, chasing a golden angel's curl, encountering a mutant Christmas tree, an endless line of waiting stars, Santa's great-great-ancestor and, of course, Father Christmas himself, sitting on a cloud under whose shadow a boy is riding down from the peaks of the Andes, spreading the news of Christ's birth ... It could be like that, but it isn't quite, maybe a little, but just maybe. An Advent calendar of Christmas short stories, profound and loving, varied and multi-faceted, presented in a wonderful narrative style that will enchant even the adult reader. A fragrance-wrapped Christmas soufflé that can be eaten over 26+1 days, on each day of Advent and Christmas plus New Year's Eve, or all at once, depending on the size of your appetite or Christmas taste ...

Roxanna
And the Mysterious Monk

Detective Roxanna has solved her first case when life, or rather death, puts another case on her desk. This brings her into contact with a wealthy English gentleman at his country estate, who has amassed a considerable fortune with an unusual business idea. Among them is a complicated hunter, who is not only a little over-the-top in his language, and especially a monk who, with his incredible intuition, not only beats the inspector to it once.

Allegories
Short Stories Volume 1 -4

The following collection in 4 volumes contains just over 60 short stories, each short story is based on a biblical passage from the New Testament like a parable and is applied to our time. A short time to catch your breath, a short time perhaps to reflect, a short time perhaps to delve deeper. Although Christ used everyday life for his parables, they still leave a deep impression today. They are easy to remember with a hidden important message that we discover when we think about them.

Uhlenspiegel with the Schilda Citizens
Volume 1 - 3

Uhlenspiegel, the lone warrior, armed with an army of mischievous thoughts, encounters a village full of Schilda citizens who are less armed, or rather, armed with different thoughts. Uhlenspiegel's premise: "Where money is at stake, it's good to be good!" And so he mischievously plays out his insights on the Schilda citizens who, with their naive way of thinking, are the appropriate antagonists. Does such an encounter make sense? Amusing and entertaining, in any case!